"Where's the Bedroom?" He Said.

His voice was low and husky in her ear.

His words brought her back to reality. She was one step away from an irrevocable act, and she panicked.

"I can't," she said.

He stared at her, breathing hard, hands on hips, much as she had seen him the day she found him exercising. But there was another reason for his breathlessness now. She looked back at him, so handsome, so desirable, that one part of her wondered how she could refuse him. But the other part, the rational one, whispered, Jenny . . . remember the last time, the hurt, the pain . . .

DOREEN OWENS MALEK

is an attorney and former teacher who decided on her current career when she sold her fledgling novel to the first editor who read it. She has been writing ever since. Born and raised in New Jersey, she has lived throughout the Northeast and now lives in Pennsylvania.

Dear Reader,

SILHOUETTE DESIRE is an exciting new line of contemporary romances from Silhouette Books. During the past year, many Silhouette readers have written in telling us what other types of stories they'd like to read from Silhouette, and we've kept these comments and suggestions in mind in developing SILHOUETTE DESIRE.

DESIREs feature all of the elements you like to see in a romance, plus a more sensual, provocative story. So if you want to experience all the excitement, passion and joy of falling in love, then SILHOUETTE DESIRE is for you

I hope you enjoy this book and all the wonderful stories to come from SILHOUETTE DESIRE. I'd appreciate any thoughts you'd like to share with us on new SILHOUETTE DESIRE, and I invite you to write to us at the address below:

Jane Nicholls
Silhouette Books
PO Box 177
Dunton Green
Sevenoaks
Kent
TN13 2YE

DOREEN OWENS MALEK
Native Season

Silhouette Desire

Published by Silhouette Books

Copyright © 1983 by Doreen Owens Malek

First printing 1984

British Library C.I.P.

Malek, Doreen Owens
  Native season.—(Silhouette desire)
  I. Title
  813'.54[F]   PS3563.A/

  ISBN 0 340 35301 5

Printed and bound in Great Britain for
Hodder and Stoughton Paperbacks, a
division of Hodder and Stoughton Ltd.,
Mill Road, Dunton Green, Sevenoaks,
Kent (Editorial Office: 47 Bedford
Square, London, WC1 3DP) by
Richard Clay (The Chaucer Press) Ltd.,
Bungay, Suffolk

For Anne Baldwin Freiberger,
companion of my childhood,
lifelong confidante.
Blessed are the peacemakers.

"Give me fullness of life like to the sun . . .
give me my inexpressible desire."

Richard Jefferies
The Story of My Heart

"To every thing there is a season,
and a time to every purpose under heaven . . .
A time to love . . ."

Ecclesiastes III: 1, 8

1

It was a beautiful midsummer morning in Philadelphia, still cool at this early hour, the sky a cloudless, pale blue. Jennifer pulled her car into the company lot and showed her pass to the security guard, who waved her on to her assigned space. She drove into it mechanically, her mind on the business of the day. It would be a long one.

She walked across the marble floor of the lobby of the Freedom Building, past the tall potted plants and the glass-enclosed business rosters on the walls. She nodded at another security guard seated at a desk and unlocked the employee elevator. Her ascent to the third floor was swift and noiseless.

Outside her office, Dolores, her secretary, handed her a stack of mail and coffee in a plastic foam cup. "Bradley Youngson at nine," Dolores reminded her, wearing a mischievous smile.

"Why the Cheshire Cat grin, Dolores?" Jennifer said, depositing her purse and the correspondence on her desk.

Dolores paused in the doorway, her smile widening. "You'll know when you see him. He was here last week when you were in Chicago." She rolled her eyes. "Sexy as hell."

"Thank you, Dolores, for that capsule assessment," Jennifer said dryly. "I only hope he can read."

Jennifer was the publicity director for the Philadelphia Freedom football team and was responsible for the contracted promotional appearances the players made on behalf of the club. In her previous dealings with the athletes she had found quite a few of them, to put it charitably, something less than bright.

"When you look like him," Dolores said, "it doesn't matter if you can read, write, or even think. The world will beat a path to your door."

Jennifer gave Dolores a look that sent her scuttling back to her typewriter. Dolores had an unfortunate tendency to moon over the more attractive players. She was otherwise an excellent secretary, but her sophomoric hero worship made Jennifer feel like the den mother at a sorority house. She was always sending Dolores off on a manufactured errand to prevent her staring, thunderstruck, at some gloriously healthy young quarterback who had arrived to sign papers. Judging by this preview, Jennifer might have to give her a one-way ticket to the Ozarks while Youngson was around.

Jennifer sat and sipped her coffee, reviewing the material on Youngson. He was an American Indian, raised on a reservation in Montana, whose athletic prowess in the school there won him a scholarship to Cornell. He had been a star halfback in college and had signed with the Green Bay Packers upon graduation. He had had a magnificent career since, at the top of the league in yardage gained and passes received wherever he had played. He had been brought to the Freedom with the publicity of an astronaut returning from Jupiter. His salary could feed the population of China for a decade, and that

did not include the perks—the cars, the clothes, the
residuals from advertisements. The man was loaded.
Jennifer always found herself resenting the amount
these players were paid, but Youngson was in a class
by himself. And all for playing a children's game.

Jennifer was not impressed. She knew the type, all
brawn and no brains. She had been married to one
of them for three years. College degrees meant
nothing in this business. Athletes were supplied with
free tutoring in order to pass the most basic courses.
And there had been more than one scandal about
grade fixing and credit given for classes never attended, so that the starting lineup would be eligible to
play. Jennifer had met some of the products of this
system: college graduates who were functional illiter-
ates, reading on a fourth- or fifth-grade level, unable
to decipher the material she handed them. She knew
that quite a few of the faces she saw grinning from
the sports pages couldn't read the stories written
about them. It had a tendency to dim the brightness
of their accomplishments on the field.

When Dolores buzzed her at 8:58, she was prepared for more of the same. At least he was on time.

"Mr. Youngson is here," Dolores said breathlessly
into the intercom.

I hope she doesn't have a heart attack, Jennifer
thought, sighing to herself. I need her for the rest of
the day. "Send him in," she said.

The door opened, Bradley Youngson entered, and
Jennifer felt her customary composure desert her.

He was tall and broad shouldered, but hadn't the
massive, hulking physique she had come to expect in
football players. He appeared to be of average
weight for his height, but his narrow waist and hips

gave him a deceptive appearance of slimness. His body was perfectly proportioned, elegant, with the pleasing symmetry of Grecian art.

Jennifer realized that she was staring and quickly dropped her eyes.

But he had caught her puzzled examination of him. "What's the matter, Ms. Gardiner?" he asked in a low, resonant voice. "Am I not what you expected?"

"I thought you would be . . . heavier," she blurted, and then closed her mouth, amazed at her loss of composure. What on earth was wrong with her? This was just another Saturday hero, another side of prime beef paid to entertain the masses with the bashing of heads. A modern gladiator in a twentieth-century arena, a member of an expensive sideshow, no more. She sat up straighter and regarded him levelly, taking a breath.

"I'm a pass receiver, Ms. Gardiner," he said with a trace of sarcasm. "I run around a lot."

She could believe that he received a lot of passes. Also that he ran around a lot.

His large, dark eyes studied her with faintly amused detachment. "You must be accustomed to dealing with linemen. They usually resemble Mack trucks."

He remained standing in front of her desk. Dolores was right. Sexy as hell. It wasn't so much his looks, though he was certainly handsome in a craggy, strong-featured way, but more a presence, a physical confidence and awareness that attracted like a magnet. Jennifer felt the pull and consciously decided to resist it.

Their eyes locked. His dusky skin had been made

even browner by the sun of a hundred football fields and had an underlying coppery tinge that bespoke his heritage. His brows and lashes were jet black, like his hair, which was beautiful, thick and straight and as glossy as a thoroughbred's coat. He stood easily, watching her, his lips slightly parted to reveal a glimpse of very white teeth.

"Please be seated, Mr. Youngson," she said stiffly.

"Call me Lee," he said, dropping gracefully into the chair across from her, stretching his long legs in front of him. He was wearing tight jeans with moccasins and a yellow V-necked sweater that clung to the muscles in his arms and shoulders and revealed the clean, supple line of his throat. He knows how to pick his colors, Jennifer thought. The bright material of his sweater was in striking contrast to his ebony eyes and hair.

Jennifer noticed that he was looking her over, too, and wondered what he thought of her. But his black gaze revealed nothing.

There was a knock at the door. Dolores opened it, simpering at Youngson.

"I just wondered if Mr. Youngson would like some coffee," she said kittenishly.

His indulgent smile suggested that Youngson was used to such fawning attention. He nodded. "Black. No sugar."

Dolores all but purred as she went out. Jennifer made a silent resolve to kill her as soon as Youngson left.

"Shall we begin?" she said pointedly to Youngson.

He raised his brows. "Please."

Jennifer handed him his copy of the typed sheets. He followed as she read the list of public appearances he was to make and explained the details involved. She took care to use the simplest language and went over each point twice.

She finished the first page. "Is there anything you would like me to explain again?" she said.

"It is not necessary to speak in words of one syllable, Ms. Gardiner," he answered quietly. "I understand."

Somewhat disconcerted, she went on. When they got to a paragraph written in legal jargon, she paused to interpret it.

He gazed at her directly across the cream bond pages in his hand. "I said I get the picture, ma'am," he said, a little more sharply.

Jennifer felt a twinge of anger. He had no right to be miffed. She was only doing her job.

"I apologize if my explanations are boring you, Mr. Youngson," she said sweetly. "I have found in the past that clearly establishing the facts saves time and effort later. While many of our clients *are* college graduates, they frequently went to school on athletic scholarships and . . ."

His jaw tightened and he pitched the papers back onto her desk. "Lady," he said, interrupting her, "I resent your attitude. I'm not a dumb jock and I'm not a dumb Indian. Maybe I went to college on a football scholarship, but I went to Cornell, which is no kindergarten. I was premed, in case the football didn't work out. I had a 3.7 average in a biology major, so please don't treat me like an idiot."

Dolores chose this inopportune moment to reenter with Youngson's drink. Her smile vanished as she sensed the atmosphere of hostility. Bewildered, she set the cup down and quickly sidled out again.

Jennifer considered what to do. She felt that she

had scored a point off him, but at the same time she was ashamed of herself. He was touchy and defensive under that gorgeous facade, and there was doubtless good reason to account for his feelings. Lord only knew what prejudices he had faced in the past. She knew that she had been condescending, and worse, it had not been entirely unintentional. His unexpected attractiveness had unnerved her, and in alarmed reaction she had struck back in the best way she knew: with the club of her intelligence.

"I'm sorry you think I was demeaning you," she said softly. "Perhaps you'd like to read the rest on your own, and let me know if you have any questions."

He relented and picked up the list again. She sat in silence as he scanned the lines. She noticed the length of his sooty lashes as his eyes moved down the sheets. He finished and handed the pages back to her. She waited.

The silence lengthened.

"Nothing to say, Ms. Gardiner?" he said, needling. "You were talkative enough before."

"You seem to find everything I say irritating," Jennifer said smoothly. "I'm trying not to annoy you."

"Is that what it is?" he responded. "I find it annoying."

Her eyes flashed to his face. It was serene, but there was a tiny hint of amusement in his eyes, a slight upward turn at the corners of his mouth. This was an overture. He would smile, if she would.

Jennifer smiled, but only slightly. He should know that she wasn't bowled over by his charm.

He grinned back at her, and she felt the full force of his considerable allure. This one was different, all right. Sharp as a scalpel and difficult to resist. She would have to be careful.

"They generally send someone along to make sure I'm a good boy on these little jaunts," he said, gesturing to the list. "Who is going to accompany me?"

"I am," she said, meeting his gaze squarely.

He sighed and stood. "Well, in that case, I suggest we forget our slight misunderstanding and begin again." He walked over to her and extended his hand. "Lee Youngson, how do you do?"

She took it. His fingers were strong and warm. "Jennifer Gardiner. Hello."

"Jennifer," he repeated, trying it out. "May I call you that?"

"Of course."

"Well, Jennifer, I'm late for practice right now, so I'd better go. I guess I'll be seeing you again."

She nodded. "On the eighteenth, for the mall opening. I'll contact you."

"Good-bye, then." His smile was touched with irony. "It was nice . . . wrestling with you."

He walked soundlessly to the door and left.

Wrestling, Jennifer thought. That was as good a term as any for what they'd been doing.

Working with Bradley Youngson was certainly going to be interesting.

2

It was a month before Jennifer saw Lee Youngson again. During that time she did her best to forget him, but to no avail. He was the darling of the newspapers, and as she was responsible for reviewing all his press releases, and even composing some of them, ignoring his existence was not possible. His performance in the practices and the preseason games was the subject of much discussion, and there was speculation about whether or not he was worth his astronomical salary. The general consensus seemed to be that he was. Jennifer found that difficult to believe. As far as she was concerned, in order to deserve what the management was paying him, he would have to cure lepers and walk on water.

One hot afternoon in mid-August Jennifer paused in the middle of dictating a batch of letters and retreated to the rest room for a few minutes of peace. There was so much to be done in preparation for the new season that the bathroom was virtually the only place where she could escape the constant demands on her attention. She drew the line when Dolores tried to follow her in with her note pad. Dolores retreated, grumbling, to her desk.

Jennifer surveyed herself in the full-length mirror and wished she were in Greenland. Or Oslo, Norway. Anyplace cool and quiet where they had never even heard of football. Every year the September zaniness got worse, and now it was beginning in July. Autumn had always been her favorite season, but since coming to the Freedom her thoughts of it were always mixed with visions of constantly ringing phones and a desk buried under piles of correspondence.

Jennifer brushed out her shoulder-length, honey-blond hair and reflected that she looked tired. There were shadows under her gray-blue eyes, and her fair skin had the drawn quality she associated with late nights reading contracts and publicity fillers. She didn't notice that her tall, slim figure was flattered by the blue silk jersey dress she wore, and her legs were long and elegant in sheer hose and heeled pumps. She reapplied a light coral lipstick and tied the sash at her waist in a neater knot. She sprayed herself with a spritz of perfume from the tiny atomizer in her purse and felt better.

She emerged to find Lee Youngson lounging against the wall outside her office. She stopped, startled. Then she glanced at Dolores, who shrugged slightly and gave her a "your guess is as good as mine" look.

The minute Jennifer saw him she knew that she had not imagined the electricity of their first encounter. During the intervening time she had tried to tell herself that her memory had magnified it, but this fiction was exploded the instant he straightened and met her glance. She felt the warmth of his eyes on her like a palpable thing. Nothing had changed.

"Hi," he said. "Got a minute?"

"Hello, Lee," she responded, schooling herself to react casually. "Sure I do. Come on in."

Jennifer turned back to Dolores, who was making faces at her over Lee's shoulder. Jennifer threw her a threatening look and shut the door.

Lee stood uncertainly, watching her. He was wearing a loosely woven cream knit top with wheat cord jeans of a slightly darker shade. He looked so vibrant, brimming with health, that he made Jennifer feel like an extreme case of vitamin deficiency. Nobody could be as fit as he seemed.

"Have a seat," she said, and he did. She noticed again his impeccable manners—he waited to be invited before he sat.

She glanced at him inquiringly.

He extracted a folded sheet of paper from his pocket. "I received this in the mail this morning," he said, rising to hand it to her.

It was the schedule for the mall opening on Saturday.

"And?" Jennifer said.

"There are a couple of things I'd like to change, if I can."

"Such as?"

"I'd like to drive myself there rather than go in the limousine. I feel like King Farouk pulling up in one of those hearses. I know where the place is, I'll be there on time."

"That's not the issue," Jennifer replied. "You are escorted for insurance reasons, as I'm sure you know. On company time, we like to take charge of your safety. Did they allow you to drive yourself when you were with the Broncos?"

He looked uncomfortable. "No, but . . ."

"You'll find that we here at the Freedom are just as cautious and solicitous of your safety as your previous employers," Jennifer said firmly.

He held up a hand. "All right, all right, I give up. I'll ride in the limo. Do you supply bulletproof vests, too?"

"Are you expecting an assassination attempt?" Jennifer countered.

They eyed each other, evenly matched, stalemated. The silence in the room lengthened.

Lee sighed. "Moving right along," he said, "do I absolutely have to spout the party line about what a great place Philadelphia is, and how happy I am to be here, and how wonderful the people are? They've heard it all before, and that kind of speech can be phoned in."

Jennifer regarded him levelly. "Let me put it this way. It wouldn't be wise to say that you hate Philadelphia and find the people obnoxious."

His eyes widened innocently. "Really? Too bad. That's just what I had in mind."

Jennifer felt the tug of war begin again.

"I think we can trust your judgment on it," she said neutrally, wanting to end the interview as soon as possible. She was growing increasingly wary— exchanging banter with him was dangerous.

"Thank you so much," he said, with exaggerated courtesy. "It's heartening to know you have such confidence in me."

"Is that all?" Jennifer said impatiently.

He stood. "That's all. I'll see you at nine-thirty on Saturday."

Jennifer nodded, watching his retreating form as he left.

Dolores materialized in the doorway seconds after he passed through it. "What was that all about?" she hissed in the tone of a conspirator.

"Dolores, don't you have *work* to do?" Jennifer asked pointedly.

"Aw, come on. Don't be a spoilsport. What did he want?"

"He just had some questions about Saturday," Jennifer said wearily. "Nothing earthshaking, I assure you."

Dolores evaluated that. "Hmm. If you ask me, he wanted to see you again."

"I'm not asking you," Jennifer said. "And besides, he'll see me on Saturday."

"Along with several hundred other people," Dolores said. "I think he wanted a cozy little tête-à-tête in your office."

"It was hardly that. We seem to get on each other's nerves. And if your theory is correct, why did he wait so long?"

"Ah-ha!" Dolores pounced. "Expecting him, were you? Disappointed that he didn't show until now?"

Mercifully, at this point the phone rang. "Will you get that?" Jennifer said in icy tones and picked up a folder, pretending to examine it.

Dolores went back to her desk, leaving Jennifer to wonder if there was any truth in what she had said.

On Saturday, the weather was stifling, so Jennifer wore a sleeveless, clinging sheath in air force blue that matched her eyes and piled her hair atop her head for coolness. She would be doing a lot of walking, so she selected shoes with a medium heel, and added a large canvas shoulder bag to hold her clipboard and other materials.

The day was overcast and humid, which made the

heat seem worse. The driver arrived for her at 9:15, and she stared moodily out the window during the drive to Youngson's condominium complex in Yardley.

The townhouses all looked the same, set decoratively amidst the exquisite plantings and immaculately landscaped lawns. There was a security station at the main gate, and Jennifer identified herself to the guard. He called ahead to Lee, who okayed their entry. Lee was waiting for them outside when they arrived.

He was wearing a navy blazer with charcoal gray slacks and a club tie. Cochise as Young Republican, Jennifer thought to herself, admitting that he had chosen well: he looked neat, conservative, and very fashionable. Damn the man. Why did she always find him so appealing?

He got into the rear seat beside her, his expression unreadable. "I hope I look okay," he said.

Jennifer turned away. He had eyes; he had mirrors. He knew how he looked. If he was fishing for a compliment, he was going to be disappointed.

"That's not for me to say," she replied stiffly.

She saw him glance at her curiously, but he kept silent.

The drive to the mall was short, for which Jennifer was grateful. The approaches to it were already jammed with traffic.

She looked at Lee, who was craning his neck unhappily. "What are all these people doing here?" he muttered. "Why aren't they home painting their garages, or something?"

Jennifer couldn't help smiling. "For the guest of honor, you are wearing a remarkably unfestive expression."

He hesitated a moment, and then said, "I don't deserve such adulation. These little kids, they should be looking up to, I don't know, Jonas Salk or Neil Armstrong or Sandra Day O'Connor. It makes me uncomfortable."

Jennifer didn't know what to say. He sounded sincere. She thought about it a moment, and then ventured, "But your manager books you for personal appearances, and you take money for doing them, don't you?"

He turned on the seat to face her. "In the first place, I don't have a manager, because I don't want one. In the second place, I only do the appearances required by my contract, like this one, and the charity stuff. That's all."

Jennifer didn't believe him. "Really?" The skepticism came through in her tone.

His lips twisted. "Really."

"What about the product endorsements, the commercials?" Jennifer persisted, knowing that she was being rude, but unable to stop herself.

He shrugged slightly. "I endorse the products I actually use, I see no harm in that. But if I think the stuff is junk, I won't go for it, no matter how much they're offering."

Jennifer wondered why he was answering her questions so readily, rather than telling her to mind her own business. He seemed to want to explain, to correct her impression of him.

"You wouldn't believe some of the approaches I've had," he added musingly. "Most of the pitches I've turned down play on my background, which I won't allow. One cooking oil outfit, which shall be nameless, wanted me to deck myself out in buckskins and a headdress and talk about how the 'braves' in my 'tribe' used to harvest the same corn used for their oil." He shook his head. "Blackfeet live in the Northwest and Canada. They harvested about as much corn as your average Eskimo. But I'll tell you something, even if my people had grown enough corn to float the continent in the stuff, I still wouldn't have done it. I'd rather hawk dog food."

Jennifer bit her lip. He had his own standards and lived up to them. That was more than could be said for most people.

The driver negotiated his way among cars until he reached one of the mall police. Then he rolled down his window and identified his passenger. The cop peered in the tinted rear window at Lee, who gave him a small half wave. The cop nodded and cleared a path for them up to the mall manager's office, where Jennifer and Lee emerged from the limousine to be shepherded inside.

They were behind the mall, out of view of the crowd, but a few stragglers still caught sight of Lee. They shouted and waved. He raised his hand in acknowledgment and kept moving. Just like royalty, Jennifer thought dryly and glanced sidelong at him. He seemed withdrawn, preoccupied. Well, he was the one who had to make the speech.

Inside, a contingent was waiting for them. It was composed of the mall manager, the general managers of the anchor department stores, the president of the development corporation that had built the mall, the local councilman, and the mayor. There was even a county beauty contest winner, complete with silken sash and rhinestone crown, who cast covert glances at Lee between pauses to adjust her banner or pat her hair into place. Lee favored them all with a practiced smile, which Jennifer could tell was trotted

out for these occasions. She had seen the real ones,
she realized: the slight, subtle curve to his mouth and
the dazzling, impish grin. This smile went with the
handshakes and the small talk and was part of his
public persona. It was genuine enough, but revealed
nothing of himself. She had seen more of the real
Lee Youngson during their two encounters in her
office than these people ever would.

The mall manager, a Mr. Vance, led them to a
central lobby where the crowd was gathered behind
ropes cordoning off the corridors. A dais, covered in
red velvet, had been placed in the center. The group
paused before reaching it and received some preliminary instructions from Mr. Vance and then proceed-
ed outside to the reviewing stand.

The mass of people erupted when they saw Lee.
He grinned and waved, taking his seat, waiting for
his introduction.

Jennifer remained at the edge of the crowd,
observing the scene.

Mr. Vance made the usual appropriate remarks,
ending with a spiel about how lucky they were to
have with them today that giant of the sports world, a
great humanitarian and a true gentleman, etc., etc.,
Lee Youngson!

Lee stepped up to the microphone during a
thunderous ovation. He lifted his arms to ask for
quiet and then launched into his talk.

Jennifer had to admire his technique. He played to
the crowd like a headliner in the Copa Room of the
Sands in Las Vegas. They hung on his every word,
laughing at his team anecdotes, listening in open-
mouthed silence to each sentence as if he were
delivering the Sermon on the Mount. She had never
seen the exercise of such power. He held them in the

palm of his hand. . . . They were his. It was a wonder to behold.

When he finished and sat again to more enthusiastic applause, the others took their turn and spoke briefly. The mayor was up last, thanking everyone as mayors generally do, and then Lee and he cut the ribbon to open the mall officially.

Jennifer watched as they posed for newspaper photographers and gave interviews to television journalists from the local stations. Jennifer listened closely to what was said and distributed releases to the reporters as they milled about the area. Lee was signing autographs and stopped to have his picture taken with his arm around the pageant winner, who smiled up at him seductively. Jennifer viewed the scene for a few moments, then looked away.

It was one in the afternoon by the time it was over, and Jennifer's feet ached from standing all that time. Lee had handled everything graciously. Why not, Jennifer thought sourly, he'd been through so many of these things he could probably do this number in his sleep. Then she felt slightly guilty at her cynicism. She could at least give him credit for a job well done.

The driver arrived to collect them shortly thereafter, and Lee slipped out a side exit with Jennifer. As they approached the waiting car he said to her, casually, "How about some lunch?"

"No, thank you," Jennifer said primly.

He glanced at her. "Why not? Aren't you hungry?"

In point of fact, she was starving. "I'd like to get home, I have a number of things to do today," she said.

"Can't they wait a little while? We'll go someplace where I won't be bothered."

"Where might that be?" Jennifer asked sarcastically. "Antarctica?"

He shot her a look and then said quietly, "Two hours, Ms. Gardiner. Is that too much to ask?"

Jennifer paused, intrigued. Why not? she reasoned. She was curious about his persistence. He seemed determined to get her to agree.

"All right," she said. "Just tell the driver where you'd like to go."

"Is that permitted?" Lee asked, smiling slightly. "I wouldn't want to break any of your rules. He can drop me back to get my own car if you think that would be advisable."

"I'll take the responsibility," Jennifer said evenly.

"Well, if you're sure," Lee answered. "I just want you to be sure."

She looked at him and saw that teasing glint in his eye.

"Mr. Youngson, I believe you're pulling my leg," she said.

"Ms. Gardiner, I'm not, but I'd love to," he replied.

Jennifer let that one pass. They got into the car and Lee instructed the driver to take them to an address in Newtown, which turned out to be a bustling, crowded Italian restaurant. Lee dismissed the driver and they approached the entrance, where a bald, rotund, middle-aged man could be seen through the plate glass window, making change at the register. Lee signalled to him from the sidewalk, and the man broke into a broad grin, collaring a younger man to take over for him and rushing outside to greet them.

"Chief! How ya doin!? Angelo wrote his mother you'd be coming out here, and then I saw it in the papers and on TV. What's happening, where ya stayin'?"

The two men had a very physical reunion, with much hugging and backslapping, and then Lee introduced Jennifer to his friend, Sal Barbetti, the owner of the restaurant. Sal's nephew, Angelo, was a second string quarterback for the Broncos, and Lee had met his family when they were out visiting Angelo.

"Hey, Chief, I never forget what you did for my boy, I mean it. Anything you want, anytime, no charge. You're always welcome here. That kid is a changed boy since, you should see him."

Jennifer glanced curiously at Lee, who was frowning at Sal, trying to make him drop the subject. Sal finally took the hint and did so, leaving Jennifer burning with the desire to know what they were talking about. But the riddle would not be solved that day. Sal hustled them around the corner of the building and took them in through the kitchen entrance, setting up a table for them in a quiet alcove behind the busboys' station. Every few minutes a dark-haired teenager would dash past in a red jacket, grabbing a tray full of glasses or a stack of dishes. Jennifer winced as she waited for a crash, but it never came. They were remarkably adept.

Sal shook out a red and white checkered table-cloth and repolished the already sparkling glassware before putting it on the table. He inspected the silverware for spots it didn't have and then pulled a paper tablet from his back pocket.

"I take your order myself, one of these idiots here might get it wrong," he said.

Lee smiled at Jennifer. "What would you like?"

"Could I have a salad?"

The owner beamed at her. "Best salad in the house, beautiful lady, plus pasta, veal scallopini or parmigiana, we got it all."

"I think just the salad."

Sal's smile faded. "What do you mean, that's all?" He stared at Lee. "What's a matter with you, Chief, you got to get this girl to eat. Look at her, she's a bone."

Lee coughed delicately, trying not to laugh. "I know, Sal, what can I tell you. Look, bring me the veal, just give the lady an antipasto, okay?"

Sal scribbled unhappily on his note pad and then seemed to have a thought which brightened him up a little. "I bring you dessert, lady," he kissed his fingers, "cannoli, tortoni, melt in your mouth, you see." He nodded, beaming, and took off to get their order.

"Wait until you see the salad he brings you," Lee grinned. "You could live off it for a week."

"What was he talking about when we first came here, something to do with his son, a favor you did for them?"

Lee made a gesture of dismissal. "Oh, don't pay any attention to that, Sal is just one of those people, heart as big as the Atlantic, effusive, eternal gratitude for any little thing you do for him, you know the type. It was nothing."

Jennifer was sure he was lying, but she didn't know why. "Do you always get such special treatment?" she asked, changing the subject.

He chuckled. "From Sal, yeah. He takes care of me."

"In other words, rank has its privileges."

Lee sobered, looking up at her. "I think it has more to do with friendship, but if you want to look at it that way, yes."

"Can't have Lee Youngson waiting around for a table with the rest of the peons," Jennifer went on.

Lee sighed. "Are you trying to pick a fight?" he asked, arching his brows.

"What's wrong, Mr. Youngson, this little luncheon date not working out the way you planned? Am I not suitably impressed? You should have asked Miss Bucks County Apple Polisher to lunch, I'm sure she would have been more congenial."

"Apple Princess," Lee corrected, amused. "And I asked *you* because I wanted to talk to *you.*"

A waiter scuttled over and deposited a carafe of ice water on the table, pausing a moment to stare at Lee.

"Talk," Jennifer said.

Lee waited until the boy had left, and then folded his arms on his chest and surveyed her critically.

"Correct me if I'm wrong, but I get the distinct impression you don't care much for me."

Nonplussed, Jennifer made no reply.

"The first time we met," he continued, "you gave me that 'you're too stupid to understand' routine, which I suspect was deliberate, and ever since then, despite a thin veneer of politeness on your part, I feel a definite chill in the air. You're only here with me right now because I practically coerced you into it. Now why is that, Ms. Gardiner?"

Jennifer studied him, weighing her answer.

He saw her indecision. "Go ahead. You can tell me," he prompted.

"I suppose I resent the amount of money you're paid to play what is essentially a children's game," Jennifer said. But she knew that wasn't the whole truth. Her calculated aloofness was a defense against the overwhelming attraction she felt for him. But it was a reasonable explanation, one he could accept.

He nodded thoughtfully. "I see."

She gestured expansively. "After all, you weren't raking in enough bucks playing for the Broncos, you had to dicker for top dollar to come here. It's difficult to read in the *Inquirer* about the millions of children starving in Asia and Africa and then turn to the sports section and see the columnists guessing at your six-figure salary."

He didn't seem angry. "You're working very hard for a fraction of what I'm making, and that bothers you. That's natural."

Sal brought their food. He placed in front of Jennifer the biggest salad she had ever seen.

"Are you sure I can't get you anything else?" he asked her anxiously.

"I'm positive. This is fine."

Sal waited until Lee had taken a bite of his veal, which was golden brown, sautéed in thin strips, delicately seasoned, as Jennifer could tell by the delicious aroma wafting across the table.

Lee made a circle of his thumb and forefinger. "It's great, Sal."

Sal was satisfied. He gave Jennifer one more wounded glance and disappeared.

"You'd better have some dessert, or he'll burst into tears," Lee warned her.

"How could I possibly eat dessert? Look at the size of this thing. It looks more like a small shrub than a salad."

"Do the best you can. Take some of it out of the bowl and distribute it around your plate."

Jennifer was arranging pieces of ham and cheese

and lettuce decoratively on Sal's china when Lee said, "Jennifer, I think you should understand something. I didn't leave the Broncos for money. The team drafted a rookie end from Northwestern who was breathing down my neck, and I didn't wait around for him to wind up standing on it. The Freedom needed me for first string. The move was made for reasons of survival, not greed."

Jennifer listened, chastened. She hadn't known about that. For the first time she realized that it must be precarious at the top—always waiting for, and fearing, the talented youngster who could come along and topple you from your perch.

"I've been playing ten years, Jennifer. Every season it's harder to get back into shape, the kids coming up look younger, the tackles are tougher to take, I can't do this forever; nobody can. The money seems like a lot, I know, but I can only earn it for a short period of time."

Jennifer had an answer for that. "But during that time, you earn more than most people do in an entire career. You can save, invest, retire, and open a chain of restaurants or become a sportscaster. Those few years set you up for life. I'll take your prospects over those of Joe Average American."

He spread his hands. "I surrender. I can't outtalk you, counselor."

Her eyes flashed to his face. "How did you know I was a lawyer?"

He smiled slightly. "Those legal terms you were rattling off when you went over my contract with me had the easy ring of familiarity. Besides, some of the mail on your desk was addressed to 'Jennifer Gardiner, J.D.' That's a law degree, isn't it?"

Jennifer eyed him. "Very observant."

He made a deprecating gesture. "I try."

Sal arrived with a pitcher of iced tea. "Fresh made, with lemon and lime," he announced. "How about some wine? Chianti, Valpolicella, Chablis, or Bordeaux for the lady?"

"No thanks, Sal. Jennifer can't get blitzed at lunch, she has a busy afternoon ahead."

Jennifer threw Lee a dirty look, to which he responded with a stare of outraged innocence.

"I bring you some garlic bread," Sal said and trudged off.

Jennifer had to laugh. "He doesn't give up easily, does he?"

Lee shook his head. "Sal is convinced that he could bring about world peace in one day if he could just get all the leaders of the various countries to sit down to a spaghetti dinner and share a few glasses of wine. What couldn't be solved under those circumstances?"

"I'm not so sure he's wrong."

Lee poured them both a tumblerful of tea. "I'm not so sure, either, counselor."

Jennifer sipped her drink. "You can drop the 'counselor.' I haven't practiced for about three years, not since I took the first contract administrator's position with the Freedom."

"Why did you leave private practice?"

"Because I was offered twice what I was making as an associate at Chaus and Reynolds to come to the Freedom."

Lee grinned. "Good reason."

"I thought so."

"But you're still a lawyer."

"I'm still a member of the bar, yes, but I don't go into court anymore. I was hired for the contracts expertise I picked up during my tenure with the firm. They did a lot of corporate work."

"I see. It's like Holy Orders, once in, never out. 'Thou art a priest forever,' that sort of thing."

He was needling her again. She decided not to rise to the bait. "In a manner of speaking, yes."

He raised his glass of tea to her and said, "Here's looking at you, kid," in a very bad Bogart imitation.

Jennifer furrowed her brow thoughtfully. "Jimmy Cagney?" she guessed.

Lee put the glass down, exasperated.

She snapped her fingers. "I know! Peter Lorre."

"Very funny," he said darkly, reaching for a breadstick. Jennifer noticed that three of the fingers on his right hand were purpled and swollen.

"Good lord," she said. "What happened to your hand?"

He glanced down at it. "Oh. I stoved my fingers in practice yesterday."

"You 'stoved' your fingers. What on earth does that mean?"

He shifted his weight back in his chair, raising his hand in the air to demonstrate. "When you catch a football, you have to palm it, like this," he said, showing her where the ball should fit into the hand of the pass receiver. "But if it's coming in too high and you try to grab it, sometimes it clips your fingers and causes bruises. It travels with a great deal of force, and the impact creates the marks you see."

"Is it very painful?"

"Oh, no. It looks worse than it is. I'd rather have this any time than a strawberry."

"A strawberry?" Jennifer asked, fascinated.

"A skin burn, similar to what baseball players get from sliding. The worst ones come from Astroturf.

They can really smart. I had one once that laid my whole arm open from the wrist to the elbow."

Jennifer listened, amazed at his tone. He spoke cheerfully, in a matter-of-fact manner that surprised her. He wasn't complaining, merely describing an occupational hazard, like a fireman discussing smoke inhalation.

Sal arrived to check on their progress. After clucking over the amount left on Jennifer's plate, he cleared the dishes away, promising to return shortly with "a surprise."

Jennifer groaned. "What does that mean? An entire sheet cake?"

"Probably. But whatever it is, please eat some of it, or I won't be responsible for the consequences."

Sal returned with a pot of espresso, a set of tiny cups and saucers, and something under a flowered napkin which he described as a "brown bonnet." He set it down and went back for dessert plates.

"Dare I take a look?" Lee said.

"Why not? Live dangerously."

Inspection revealed a round cake, iced with chocolate, with a topping of cherries in a thick glaze. When Sal came back, he sliced into it to reveal a whipped cream center.

"Here you go," he said, cutting a huge piece for Jennifer and an even huger one for Lee. "I wrap up the rest of it for you to take home."

"Thanks, Sal," Lee said, winking at Jennifer. "It looks fantastic."

"Baked this morning," Sal said proudly.

"Have some with us," Lee offered.

"Oh, no, got to get back," Sal said. "Another time, you come in, we have a good dinner, okay?"

"Okay."

Sal vanished again. They could hear him at the back of the kitchen scolding one of the waiters in staccato Italian.

Lee laughed, lifting a forkful to his mouth. "If Roy could see me with this, he'd put me on suspension for a week."

"Roy?"

"The team trainer."

"Oh, you mean Roy O'Grady."

"Yup. If I gain a pound he screams at me like an enraged leprechaun. 'You got to be thin to be fast,' he says. I often point out to him that he himself is thirty pounds overweight, but it doesn't seem to make much of an impression."

But Jennifer noticed that he only took two bites and left the rest. Self-denial had become a way of life.

They drank the coffee, and Jennifer realized that the clock on the wall behind Lee read almost four. Lee saw her glance at it and pushed his chair back. "I'll just go talk to Sal a minute. He won't let me pay for this, and he'll also want to saddle me with three salamis and a prosciutto ham before I go. I want to give him some tickets. I'll be right back."

Jennifer waited, taking out her compact and examining herself in its mirror. She looked glowing . . . happy. And she knew the reason why.

Lee returned, with a package wrapped in butcher paper under his arm. "I begged off the cake and wound up with a baked chicken instead," he said, grinning. "I also called a cab. Let's make our getaway now, before Sal sees the taxi. He'll want me to take his car."

They tiptoed out like kids playing hide and seek

and met the cab at the door. They tumbled into the back, breathless, laughing, pleased with their escape.

Jennifer gave the cabbie her address, and a silence fell as they realized their time together was coming to an end. When they pulled up to Jennifer's house, Lee told the cabbie to wait and walked her to the door.

There didn't seem to be anything to say. Their shared afternoon had changed things between them, and they both knew it.

Lee ran a strand of her hair through his fingers. "I enjoyed myself today, Jenny with the light brown hair."

"So did I."

He glanced up at the two-story frame house. "Do you live here alone?"

"I rent the second floor from the widow of a doctor. She owns the house and lives downstairs. The upper story used to be his office, and she had it converted for a rental when he died." She couldn't imagine a topic of less interest at the moment, but she was stalling and had the feeling he was, too.

"Are you going to be in that game for the Heart Fund in a couple of weeks?" he asked.

He was referring to a charity benefit that the Freedom sponsored each year as a preseason event. Some of the players participated in a touch football game with a group of employees, and tickets were sold to spectators, with the proceeds going to the Heart Fund.

"I think so," Jennifer said. "I usually go and make a fool of myself."

"I guess I'll see you then," he said.

"I guess you will."

They stared at each other. He was so close Jennifer could see the dense frame of thick dark lashes shading his eyes, a tiny mole at the edge of his upper lip, the soft, heavy sweep of the glossy black hair as it lay across his forehead. He studied her with the same intensity.

He started to speak, and for just a second Jennifer was sure he was going to ask her out socially. But he seemed to think better of it and said instead, "Good-bye, then, Jenny."

She loved the way he said her name. "Good-bye, Lee."

He trotted down the flagstone walk and paused to turn at the door of the cab. He lifted his hand in a final salute and got in.

Jennifer watched the cab until it was out of sight; then slowly, as if in a dream, she climbed the steps to the second floor and let herself into her empty apartment.

3

Jennifer had a date with John Ashford that night, but she knew that she was very inattentive company. John was an attorney with Chaus and Reynolds, and he'd remained there after she left. He had been trying to escalate their relationship into something more serious for some time now, but Jennifer was satisfied with an occasional dinner or movie. She just didn't feel the requisite degree of enthusiasm about him, and had told him so, gently, several times. As a result, he gave up in frustration about twice a year, and then wound up calling her again a few weeks later. They were currently in the middle of an "on" period, and Jennifer gave it about a month before he would pressure her and she would balk. Then he would retire in silence to pout, and the ritual would begin again. It was such a familiar scenario that by now she could almost predict when John's patience would wear thin. Jennifer felt sorry for him, but sorrier for herself. Why couldn't she fall for somebody safe, steady, and reliable like John? It would be the answer to a prayer, but she knew it would never happen. The men who attracted her were of a different strain altogether.

Jennifer looked across the restaurant table at John and compared him with the man who had shared her previous meal that day. Why didn't John's *eyes* sparkle with incipient mischief and hidden fires? Why weren't they deep and dark and full of feeling, instead of china blue and ordinary? Why wasn't his hair a rich, shiny blue-black, begging to be touched, instead of mouse brown and about as inspiring as a piece of toast? Jennifer sighed and took another bite of her steak. It wasn't John's fault. She occupied herself for the rest of the evening by reviewing the afternoon with Lee in her mind and made inane replies to John's comments to indicate that she was listening. This wasn't as successful as she'd hoped, however; she must have shown her distraction because she caught John looking at her oddly several times, and when he took her home, he didn't try to worm his way inside as he usually did. He gave up without a struggle and left her to her thoughts.

Jennifer changed to a robe and made a cup of tea, taking it into the living room and curling up on the couch. The steam from the cup drifted past her eyes as she sat motionless, seeing again Lee's smiling face. The reason for her wariness of him was no mystery. He reminded her too much of Bob.

Jennifer had met Bob Delaney when he was a rookie shortstop for the Phillies and she was a freshman in law school. She had attended a workshop on the legal representation of professional athletes, and Bob had been one of the speakers. Immediately taken by his good looks and easy charm, Jennifer found herself married to him three months later.

It wasn't long before the bloom was off the rose. Stories of Bob's infidelities on road trips and tours drifted back to her when they had been together less than a year. And that wasn't all. He had a drinking problem; often he was too hung over to play and began accumulating fines and suspensions like parking tickets. Jennifer blamed herself as well as Bob for the failure of their marriage. If she had taken the time to see what he was really like before rushing headlong into a commitment, she would have realized that they could never make a go of it. Well, she wasn't going to make the same mistake twice.

The similarities between Lee and her ex-husband were too numerous to list. That same dazzling sex appeal, which in Bob's case concealed a character as shallow as a tide pool, the same slender, graceful athlete's body, the personal magnetism, and the effortless, winning way. The flaws didn't show for a while in the wash of the sun, but sooner or later, the clouds gathered, and then the cracks in the facade began to appear. Jennifer knew it all too well.

She sipped her tea and stared morosely at the pattern in the rug. So I'm a sucker for charismatic jocks, she thought. And I'm in the wrong business, because sooner or later I was bound to run across another one.

And sooner or later, she had.

I mustn't panic, she mused. Lee doesn't know how I feel. He's got a lot going for him, but as far as I know he can't read minds. If I just watch myself, take extra care when I'm around him, he'll never guess and I'll be safe.

Comforted by that thought, she switched on the television and lost herself in the Saturday night movie.

On Sunday afternoon, Jennifer drove to her friend Marilyn's apartment for dinner. Marilyn lived in a garden apartment complex in Ewing, N.J., which

was a suburb of Trenton and just across the Delaware
river from Jennifer's home in Yardley, Pa.

Jennifer and Marilyn had been friends for years,
since meeting in college when they were paired off as
lab partners in a chemistry course. The relationship
got off to a volatile start when Jennifer had ignited
the fumes from Marilyn's beaker of ether. Marilyn
had been the maid of honor at Jennifer's wedding,
and Jennifer was the godmother of Marilyn's son,
Jeff.

Marilyn had gone back to teaching when her
husband, an insurance agent, had been killed in an
automobile accident two years before. He had fallen
asleep at the wheel on the way home from a
convention and crashed into a utility pole. Jeff was
three at the time.

Jennifer and Marilyn had helped each other a
great deal during their respective crises, and Jennifer
trusted Marilyn's judgment and opinion more than
anyone else's. So she was glad that she would see
her that day—she could use a heavy dose of
Marilyn's common sense and natural optimism.

Jeff hurled himself at her when she came through
the door, and she spent the first few minutes of her
visit listening with rapt attention to the kindergarten
news. When they had exhausted the topics of show
and tell and acrobatic arithmetic (which was apparently some game his teacher had invented), he took
himself off to watch television and Marilyn called
Jennifer into the kitchen.

Jennifer followed the aroma of fresh coffee and
paused at the table, where Marilyn was basting the
hem of a skirt, her mouth full of pins.

"Help yourself," Marilyn muttered, and Jennifer
poured out two cups, getting the cream from the

refrigerator and the sugar from the cupboard shelf. She sat across from her friend, and Marilyn studied her absorbed expression for a while in silence.

"All right, out with it," Marilyn finally said, after removing the pins from her mouth and sticking them in a cushion. "What trouble is furrowing that noble brow?"

"No trouble."

"Hmph. That was said with all the sincerity of Eddie Haskell complimenting Mrs. Cleaver on her wardrobe."

Jennifer laughed. She and Marilyn shared a passion for old TV shows and identified more with Lucy Ricardo and Ethel Mertz than any of the characters currently populating the tube. While everybody else in the college dorm had slept in on Saturday morning, she and Marilyn had been up to catch the reruns of "I Love Lucy."

"That's not an answer," Marilyn said.

Jennifer stirred her coffee with more vigor than was necessary. "I had lunch with Lee Youngson yesterday," she said casually.

Marilyn was instantly alert. "That ballplayer? The Indian who just came to the Freedom this year?"

"That's the one."

Marilyn nodded slowly. "I saw him on the news when he signed his contract. He looked like Atahualpa come to life, all gleaming teeth and magnificent bone structure. Is he that picturesque in person, too?"

"More so."

Marilyn's hand froze in the act of reaching for the sugar bowl. "Oh-oh. I don't like this. You've got that Bob Delaney look on your face again, Jen, and you know what that means."

"I know what that means," Jennifer repeated miserably.

"Did anything happen?" Marilyn asked, worried.

"Oh, no, of course not, I just met the man. But he's going to be around all year, and I have a feeling I'm in for a long siege."

Marilyn filled a teaspoon with sugar and then sifted some of it back into the bowl before adding the rest to her cup. "Has he asked you out yet?"

"No. I thought that he was on the verge of doing so yesterday, but he seemed to decide against it."

"Uh-huh. You're sure you weren't giving off negative vibrations at the time?"

Jennifer thought back to the scene when Lee had left her, the two of them unable to say anything intelligent, unable to part, either "No, I would say that the vibes were very positive."

"Then," Marilyn supplied. "But what about the rest of the day?"

"Well, I did give him a bit of a hard time at lunch," Jennifer admitted.

"I'll bet you did," Marilyn said. "Can you wonder that the poor guy is confused?"

"'The poor guy,' as you put it, is probably working on the third edition of his little black book right now, and is hardly lamenting his lack of success with me. Judging by the reaction of Dolores and the other women I've seen in his presence, they drop like flies at an encouraging word."

Marilyn nodded sagely. "It seems to me I've heard this song before," she said. "As I recall, you said the same thing about Bob Delaney."

Jennifer drained the last of her coffee. "You're right. I can't fall into that trap again."

"Take it one step at a time," Marilyn advised,

standing and turning on the oven to preheat it for the roast: "If he's interested, he'll let you know."

"If *he's* interested! I don't know if *I'm* interested."

Marilyn favored her with a knowing look. "Ask me. I'll tell you. It's written all over your face."

Jennifer said nothing.

"Be careful, Jen," Marilyn said seriously. "Don't set yourself up for another fall."

"Don't worry," Jennifer said. "I won't."

She meant it.

Jennifer buried herself in her work for the next two weeks, and successfully kept Lee Youngson out of her mind. She was flicking through the channels once on television, stopped short when she saw him being interviewed by a local sportscaster, and then forced herself to switch to another show.

The Friday afternoon before the benefit game, Jennifer drove out to Westminster State College, where the Freedom had its summer camp, with a stack of papers for some of the players to sign. They had to be in the house mail on Monday morning, and the athletes were notoriously unreliable about getting things in on time, so Jennifer decided not to take any chances. She set out for the school right after lunch.

It was a beautiful drive along the Philadelphia main line, and Jennifer enjoyed the scenery and the colonial landmarks along the way. It wasn't long before she was pulling into one of the parking lots, scanning the practice field unconsciously for a glimpse of Lee. Her car made a curious whining sound as the motor died, and she frowned in momentary concern, but was too preoccupied with the business at hand to give it much thought.

Jennifer walked out to the bleachers and asked one of the assistant coaches how long it would be before the team took a break. He looked at his watch and guessed about ten minutes. She sat on the bottom step and prepared to wait. They were currently on the system of "two a day," which meant a practice from nine to eleven, a break until one, and then another practice in the afternoon. She would have to stick around until they paused in the middle of the second session. Nothing, short of a bomb falling, was permitted to interrupt the work at hand.

She was the only woman in sight. Usually her appearance occasioned a few wolf whistles and catcalls, but the players were too absorbed in their practice to notice her arrival. She sat quietly and watched the various drills going on, which included her favorite, the "stomp" drill. During this exercise the team members ran in place as fast as possible, drumming their feet on the ground, and never failed to remind her of a crowd of oversized babies having a simultaneous tantrum.

After a few minutes they split up, and Jennifer spotted Lee sprinting to the backfield with the quarterback, Joe Thornridge, a lanky kid two years out of Auburn. Joe was known as "Thunderbolt Thornridge" for the speed and accuracy of his passes. Lee was his favorite target, and as Jennifer watched the two men working out together, it was easy to see why. They moved with the intricate, perfectly timed synchronization of a Swiss watch. Again and again Lee took off down the field, and Joe rolled back, arm cocked behind his head, and fired off a pass that dropped into Lee's waiting hands as if it were an apple falling off a tree. They made it look so easy, but

Jennifer knew it wasn't. These two would not be collecting the paychecks they were if everybody could do it.

Lee was wearing the bottom part of an old uniform, complete with pads, and an ancient, ragged T-shirt, dampened now under the arms and in the hollow of his back from his exertions. Jennifer found herself wishing that he would take it off, and then shook her head, angry with herself. That sort of thinking was guaranteed to get her nowhere, fast.

When the head coach blew his whistle and the team members filed slowly off the field, Jennifer opened her briefcase and took out the documents that needed signatures. Out of the corner of her eye she saw Lee take a dipper of water from the container on the bench, swish it around in his mouth, and then spit it out. He stretched his arms over his head, the muscles flexing across his back under the clinging shirt. Deliberately, she turned her head.

She managed to find all but one of the players she needed to see. Roy O'Grady told her that the missing man had been taken to a specialist for an examination for a possible torn ligament, but would be back by the end of the practice. Frustrated, Jennifer realized that she would have to hang around until the man returned. Well, she certainly wasn't going to sit in the stands like some gawking groupie and watch Lee Youngson perform. She decided to take a drive and return when the time was right to see the last player and finish the job.

This idea was abandoned when she couldn't get her car to start. All she heard when she turned the ignition key was an ominous grinding noise.

Sighing, she walked back to the field and asked

where there was a phone that she might use. She was directed inside the administration building of the college, where there was a pay phone in the lobby.

Jennifer had no idea which garage to call, since the one she usually used was twenty miles away, and she was not familiar with any in Westminster. There was a telephone book attached to the booth by a chain, and she picked a name out of the yellow pages, dialing with one hand and searching for her VISA card with the other. She had exactly fifteen dollars in cash and the strong feeling that it wouldn't be enough to cover a fraction of what this would cost her.

It took her three tries before she could get a garage to send a mechanic out to her location, and then she waited thirty minutes for him to arrive.

The person who finally showed up looked as though he should be incarcerated in a home for wayward boys. A pimply teenager in filthy overalls with a two days' growth of scraggly beard, he took a bigger interest in Jennifer than in the state of her malfunctioning car. He stared at her legs while she tried to explain what had happened, and then stuck his head under the hood and poked a few things with a selection of greasy tools he had brought with him. Jennifer stood anxiously nearby, wondering how long this was going to take.

He straightened and turned to face her. "Lady, this car has got to be towed. We can send somebody out for it later, and I can give you a ride back to the station in the truck."

That suggestion had little to recommend it. The truck wasn't in much better shape than its driver, and an excursion in the country with this lecherous adolescent wasn't exactly what Jennifer had in mind. She was hesitating, trying to decide what to do, when she heard voices behind her.

The practice had broken up, and the players were heading out to their cars. She saw Lee, walking in a group of three, talking to a husky guy at his side who was gesturing in the air, obviously delivering a punchline. Lee laughed, and turned his head, catching sight of Jennifer. He stopped, and she saw him say something to his companions, who then followed his progress towards Jennifer with their eyes.

Lee took in the scene at a glance. "Hi, Jen," he said. "What's going on?"

Jennifer was ashamed of how glad she was to see him. She had thought she was long past the point where she had to depend on a man to solve her problems, but Lee as an alternative to Greasy George was a no-choice situation. Lee would help her.

"My car broke down, and the garage sent this man to take a look at it."

Lee took his wallet out of his pocket and handed the boy a folded bill before Jennifer could protest. "Thanks for coming out," he said. "I'll take care of this now."

The boy shrugged and shambled off toward his truck. Lee turned his attention to Jennifer.

"How've you been, paleface?" he asked, slamming the hood of her car. "Aside from this encounter with Tony's Garage, that is."

"I wonder if that was Tony," Jennifer said. "He doesn't look old enough to drive."

"Or clean enough," Lee added, and Jennifer smiled.

"That's better," Lee said. "Now let's see what we can do about this car."

He was pulling his own keys from his pocket when a black Corvette cruised past with two of Lee's teammates in the front seat.

"Look out, Chief," one of them yelled.

The other whistled shrilly and gave Lee the high sign, cackling madly. Then the driver honked the horn and the car sped away on screeching tires.

Lee shook his head, and Jennifer could have sworn there was a faint tinge of red sweeping up his neck under that dusky skin. "Those guys," he said. "I keep hoping they'll grow up, but they keep disappointing me."

"Why do they call you 'Chief'?"

He looked at her as if she'd lost her mind. "Because I'm Norwegian, Jennifer."

Jennifer swallowed and tried again. It had come out wrong, the way everything always seemed to when she tried to talk to him.

"I meant, why do you let them call you that? I would have thought you wouldn't like it."

He glanced at her curiously. "Why wouldn't I like it? They're my friends. I'm not some hypersensitive loony with a chip on my shoulder, Jennifer. It only bothers me when I think somebody is trying to put me down because I'm an Indian."

"The way you thought I was when we first met," Jennifer said, before she considered it. Then she bit her lip. She hadn't wanted to remind him of that.

But he only smiled slightly. "That's right." He lounged back against the door of her car and folded his arms. "But now you can call me Chingachgook or Running Water for all I care."

Jennifer laughed, and he leaned forward to tilt her chin up with a long, brown forefinger. "Just as long as you call me."

She sobered and stared into his searching, depthless eyes. The shouting and horseplay of the departing players faded into the background, and it was as if they were alone in the parking lot. She wanted to kiss him, had to restrain herself from doing so then and there, with all of his teammates milling around them. And he knew it. His eyes became heavy lidded, slumberous, and his lips parted, as if in anticipation of a caress.

"Hey, Chief, you posin' for a statue?"

The voice rang out behind them, and they sprang apart guiltily, as if caught in some misdeed. The Freedom's quarterback sauntered up to them, grinning widely.

"Jennifer, I'd like you to meet Joe Thornridge, my bodyguard," Lee said sarcastically. "He substitutes for my mother when she isn't available to keep an eye on me. Joe, Jennifer Gardiner."

Joe stuck his hand out to Jennifer, whose small one was lost in his huge, meaty palm. "How do, ma'am?" Joe said in a thick Southern accent. "I've seen you at the offices. Pretty hard to miss, I'd say. And I met your secretary, Dolores."

I'll bet you did, Jennifer thought with amusement.

"You better watch out for the Chief, here, little lady," Joe said warningly. "He's got all those fancy moves, ya know? If you need anybody to take over for him, somebody a little safer, say a Southern gentleman, you just let me know."

Jennifer smiled. "I'll keep it in mind."

"I think your wife is calling you, Joe," Lee said.

Joe sent Lee a wounded look.

"Scram, kid," Lee said.

Joe slung his duffel bag over his shoulder and ambled off, caroling, "Remember what I said," back to Jennifer.

"I'll remember," she answered.

"I'd forget, if I were you," Lee said darkly. "He's got two kids already and a pregnant wife."

Jennifer glanced at him, amazed. He was only half kidding. Could he possibly be jealous? Joe had only indulged in some good-natured teasing. There was no reason for Lee's testy reaction.

They were alone in the lot now; the last of the men had left when Joe did.

"Well, I guess we'd better see about this car," Lee announced and turned to walk around it. His legs suddenly buckled under him and Jennifer had to rush to catch him, to keep him from falling to the ground.

Despite his slim appearance, he was quite heavy, and she staggered under his weight. He clutched at her, and she eased him against the rear fender of her car.

"That's one of my fancier moves," he grunted. "Trick knee, it gives out on me at the damndest times."

He was speaking directly into her ear, draped over her for support. As she stepped back, he held her, pulling her into his arms.

This was their first real physical contact, and it completely unraveled Jennifer. His body was lean, hard, and totally male. He ran his hands down her arms and across her back, molding her to him. She resisted the strong impulse to cling and refused to allow herself to melt into him. When he saw that she was not going to cooperate, he released her, and she moved away from him, flustered.

"Are you all right now?" she asked faintly.

"I was better a minute ago," he answered, referring to their impromptu embrace.

Jennifer wouldn't discuss it. As far as she was concerned, it had been a mistake.

"What causes that to happen?" she asked, moving to lock the doors of her car.

He had no choice but to follow. "I've had three operations on that knee in five years," he replied. "At this point, it's held together with chewing gum. I just have to move the wrong way, and it collapses."

"Does it give way during games?" she asked.

"Sure does," he answered. "Especially since the other team knows it's a weak point and aims straight at it. That's why there are always a lot of clipping fouls against me."

"Clipping?"

He demonstrated. "When someone is going to tackle you, he comes in like this," he said, lowering his head and aiming for her legs. "But if he catches you in the back of the knees, it's a violation, called clipping." He made a chopping motion, as she had seen referees do during games. "With me, they're always trying to nail that bad knee, and yet keep it legal at the same time, which is very hard to do."

Jennifer absorbed this in silence. My God, he was going into each game just waiting for a bunch of gorillas to launch themselves at him, like a human target on a firing range. Up to this point, she hadn't thought of football players as especially courageous, but it took guts to do what he did every week of the season.

He read her expression. "Don't worry, paleface.

You're looking at one tough Injun. My people survived massacres, disease, westward expansion, and the reservation system. The NFL isn't going to do me in."

Jennifer rolled up the last window and slammed the door. "What do you suggest doing about this?" she asked, jerking her thumb at the car.

"I'll give you a ride, and I'll call my garage in Yardley to come and get it."

"Will they come so far?"

He smiled grimly. "For me they will. I just spent a small fortune there on my wheels. They'd better not say no."

He opened the passenger door of his car for Jennifer and leaned in past her to shift some papers off the seat. His nearness set her pulse racing again. She waited until he got in beside her and said, to cover her nervousness, "What type of Indian are you?"

He arched an eyebrow at her, starting the car. "Type?"

Why did she always say the wrong thing? "Tribe, clan, I guess I don't know the right word."

"Blackfoot," he said. "It's part of the Algonquian nation."

Ah, yes. She remembered that the sportswriters sometimes referred to him as the "Blackfoot Bullet." Also the "Cawassa Comet." They were very fond of tag lines.

"What does Cawassa mean?" she asked.

"It's the town in Montana where I was born, on the reservation, about three miles northwest of Browning."

"What language is that?"

"Pikuni. It's a dialect of Ojibwa, spoken by the

Blackfeet in that region, in the Northwest, and in Canada in the area of Lake Superior."

"Ojibwa?"

He grinned. "Are you writing a book?"

Jennifer flushed, embarrassed. "I'm sorry. I'm asking too many questions."

He put the sports car in gear and drove out of the lot. "Don't be silly. I'll tell you anything you want to know. I just couldn't resist teasing you a little. You get so rattled, like a fourth-grade genius who missed the last word in the spelling bee."

Jennifer giggled. He was right.

"Now, in answer to your last question, Ojibwa is the mother language of the Algonquian tribes; it's more often called Ottawa or Chippewa."

"Yes, I've heard those terms."

"It's rather like Castilian Spanish, with Pikuni the equivalent of an Andalusian variant. They're about as similar as modern Polish and Czech. I grew up speaking Pikuni, but I can follow a conversation in Ojibwa."

"I see."

"And 'Ojibwa' itself means 'to roast until puckered up,' which is a reference to the puckered seams on Blackfoot moccasins."

"No kidding? What an odd way to get a name."

He cast her a sidelong glance. "I hope you're paying attention, because there's going to be a test."

Jennifer laughed, thinking that she had already had one test that day, when he had held her in his arms. She had passed it. This time.

He asked whether she would like to go home, or back to the office, and regretfully she told him to take her to the office. She still had to try to get in touch with the last player who hadn't signed his papers.

Lee asked her why she had come to practice that day, and she explained the situation.

"Give that stuff to me," he said. "I'll see that Roger signs it and returns it to your office on Monday."

"Would you do that? It would be a big help. Otherwise I'll be trying to track him down for the rest of the weekend."

"No problem. Still want to go back to the office?"

"I'm afraid so. That wasn't the only thing I have left to do."

He nodded and took the turnoff for Philadelphia.

They were back to the Freedom's offices too soon. Jennifer could remember every word of their conversation in vivid detail—she felt as if it had been burned into her brain. It wasn't particularly stimulating or witty, but she had shared it with Lee, and for that reason it was important to her.

Lee pulled to a stop outside the building. "Here you are," he said. "Back the same day."

"I can't thank you enough for your help. And I owe you the money you gave that boy from Tony's Garage."

"Forget it. It was my pleasure. I'll have the mechanic at my garage get in touch with you about the repairs."

"Fine. And thanks again."

He tossed his fingers in a tiny salute and drove off. Jennifer went into the lobby in a daze, filled with thoughts of Lee.

The Sunday of the benefit game for the Heart Fund was clear and cooler than it had been, a precursor of fall. Jennifer arrived just as it was beginning, wearing Marilyn's jogging suit and an apprehensive smile. She didn't expect this to be her finest hour.

Dolores was waiting for her on the sidelines. "The first team is already in," she said. "They're going to start in a moment."

"Good. I hope they never get around to me."

"They will," Dolores said cheerfully. "Tom said everybody will see some action, if only for a few minutes."

"Great." Tom was an accountant in payroll, and he was managing the roster.

Jennifer shielded her eyes as she watched the action on the field. Lee and Joe Thornridge and a few others were out there, along with the cream of the Freedom's amateur athletes. The crowd was large and vocal, screaming every time anybody made a move.

She and Dolores watched the game for a while, sipping soft drinks and surveying the onlookers wandering around Westminster's campus.

It wasn't long before Tom was waving at Jennifer, signaling her to join the players on the field.

"Every year I tell him I don't know how to play this game," she muttered.

"And every year he ignores you," Dolores responded. "I know, I know. Go on, it can't be any worse than last time."

The "last time" Jennifer had crashed into the team bench while trying to catch the ball and gave Esther Lopinsky, one of the secretaries, a black eye.

Jennifer ran onto the field and watched nervously as Leo Smithers, the quarterback of the staff team, signaled her to come and talk to him.

"On the next play," he said, "I'm going to pass the ball to you."

"Uh, I don't think that's such a good idea, Leo," she said.

"Why not?"

"Because I don't know what to do with it once I get it, that's why not."

He rubbed his eyes wearily with his thumb and forefinger. "Look, Jen, all you have to do is try to catch the ball, and then run as hard as you can in that direction," he instructed, pointing toward the goalpost at the end of the field. "Everybody else knows what they have to do. So don't worry about it, okay? Just grab it and try to cross the line at the end."

Leo called for a huddle, in which various team members said things Jennifer didn't understand. But she kept Leo's words in mind and stood where he placed her at the lineup.

She saw Lee, drooped in faded jeans and a white knit skivvy, watching her across the line of scrimmage. That didn't make her feel any better.

Leo called out a series of numbers, and then faded back for the pass. Jennifer started to run, looking over her shoulder for the ball, hoping that Leo's confidence in himself was justified and that he would be able to "hit her" no matter what she did.

When it became obvious that he was throwing to her, players from the pro club materialized from nowhere, heading in her direction. Terrified, she looked up to see the ball hurtling through the air toward her.

How did anybody ever catch these things? They were an impossible shape. She grabbed for it, got her fingers on the edge, and then it squirted out of her hands. She leaped after it and managed to catch it. At that moment Lee caught her about the knees and tumbled her gently to the ground.

Jennifer landed on her dignity, and then was up in a flash, yelling at the top of her lungs.

"Wait a minute! This is supposed to be touch football. That's illegal, you can't tackle anybody in this game!"

The onlookers were delighted. They stamped their feet and clapped, roaring their approval. Lee stood by, looking mysteriously smug, and hung his head when the referee came over to give him a tongue lashing. Jennifer told Tom to replace her and walked off the field.

The nerve of him, pouncing on her like that. She retied her sneakers, sitting on the staff bench, yanking at the laces viciously. When she raised her head again, Lee was standing in front of her.

"They threw me out of the game," he said happily.

Jennifer stared at him, the light beginning to dawn. "You did that deliberately," she said.

"Pure reflex. Couldn't help myself."

"I'll bet."

"However, since we both seem to be at liberty, why don't we take a stroll around the grounds?"

"Stroll alone. After that little stunt I wouldn't go around this bench with you."

His face changed. "What's the matter? You're not hurt, are you?"

"Only my pride."

He smiled engagingly, and she could feel her resistance melting away under the force of his charm. "Come on. This thing is going to be breaking up in another half an hour or so, and then they're having a picnic. We'll come back and get something to eat later."

The desire to be with him overrode her previous

annoyance. "I'm doing this against my better judgment," she warned him. "The minute I lower my guard you'll probably blindside me again."

"Sounds tempting," he said, motioning with his head toward the grassy copse beyond the playing field. "Let's go. I'll tell you about my great-grandfather, the shaman. That should interest a student of Indian folklore like yourself."

It did. "What's a shaman?"

"A medicine man, a caster of spells and a weaver of charms. Combination faith healer, herbalist, and grass-roots psychologist."

They were walking away from the crowd, and the game noises faded in the distance. The sun was warm, and Lee pulled his shirt over his head to reveal a sleeveless tank top underneath. He spread the skivvy on the ground and gestured for her to sit on it. She did, and he sprawled full length beside her. A screen of trees blocked them from view.

"What kind of charms did your great-grandfather weave?"

"All kinds. Love charms, hate charms, charms to make you sick, charms to make you well. His specialty was healing, though. He would put on his saamis, the medicine hat, with feathers and magical bones, and cure anything that ailed you. He died when I was twelve."

Too bad he's not around today, Jennifer thought. I could use a little help in curing myself of my growing infatuation with you. She stretched out on the grass and sighed.

Lee rolled over on his stomach and the sun glinted off his shining, coal-black hair, making it glow with highlights.

"That old man, he knew something, something

that's been lost forever now," Lee said softly. "And I don't think it's possible to get it back."

"I understand what you mean," Jennifer replied. "That knowledge the old people had, I think we traded it for jet planes and microwave ovens and potato chips in à tennis ball can. And I'm not sure we're better off now. The problems aren't solved; they're only different."

Lee pushed himself up on his forearms and gazed down into her face. "I think you're a very smart lady," he said.

"Thank you, kind sir," she answered, smiling. Her smile faded slowly as she met his gaze and awareness grew between them. Jennifer was very conscious of his almost naked torso above her, the proximity of that powerful, agile body. She tried to sit up, and he pinned her, holding her arms and leaning into her. Prone, submissive, she could feel the warmth of his skin against hers, his breath fanning her cheek. The black eyes seared hers. Then his lashes obscured them as his face came closer and he lowered his mouth to hers.

The kiss began tentatively, as all first kisses do, but it was only seconds before Jennifer was kissing him back passionately. She had known all along that she desired him, but the abstract idea was nothing compared with burning reality. His mouth was wonderful, drugging, sensitive and mobile, and a treasure of delights to explore. His tongue probed hers, and she yearned against him, eager for more.

"I've wanted to do that since the moment I met you," he murmured, moving his mouth to her ear, and then back to her lips. He adjusted his position to lie more fully against her, and she gasped as she felt him, ready, against her thigh. His hands slid underneath her to press her to him, and she clasped her arms around his neck.

He raised his head and looked around, and Jennifer realized with alarm that he was checking to see if anyone was watching them, if it was safe to make love to her there, hidden in the small, enclosed wood.

Jennifer began to struggle. The man was mad. If he thought she would be a partner to an outdoor romp in the middle of a park, he was in for a rude awakening.

"Let me go," she demanded, and he released her instantly, rolling off her. She struggled to her feet, brushing bits of leaves and grass and other debris from her clothes. She felt ridiculous, ashamed.

He stood also, with his hands jammed in his pockets, his hair falling forward over one eye.

"What are you so upset about?" he asked. "I kissed you. You kissed me back."

Of course, Jennifer thought. He did this sort of thing all the time.

"Why did you push me away?" he wanted to know.

"You may be in the habit of casual rolls in the hay during coffee breaks, but I certainly am not," Jennifer said.

His eyes narrowed. "Is that what you think?" he asked. "That I was promoting a pleasant interlude until it's time to dish up the potato salad? Grab you, and then grab a hamburger?"

Jennifer's silence was his answer.

He was starting to look very upset. His eyes were flashing sparks, and she could see that the hands in his pockets were balled into fists.

"I seem to have misjudged the situation here," he said softly.

"That makes two of us," Jennifer replied nastily.

"Always the smart comeback," he said. "You'd better watch out, counselor; if you're that sharp, you'll cut yourself."

Jennifer stared at him, then opened her mouth to speak, but nothing happened.

He held up a hand. "Let me say it for you," he intoned. "You think I'm a lowlife and a user, and the sight of me makes you sick. That about cover it?"

She dropped her eyes. The sight of him could never make her sick.

"I'll see you later, Jennifer. I think I'd better exit before I say something I'll regret."

Jennifer didn't look up until he was gone.

She spent the weeks following the picnic in a state of suspended animation, hoping for a glimpse of Lee and dreading it at the same time. Her fears were groundless. She never saw him and finally concluded that he was avoiding the Freedom's offices. She knew she was right when she learned that he had had several things delivered there by messenger. He was taking no chances of running into her.

It was amazing how dull everything seemed now, without him. Events that once would have delighted her provoked little reaction. She had lunch with Harold Salamone, the owner of the Freedom, to discuss some business, which was unprecedented, and it did nothing to lift her spirits. At any other time such recognition would have left her elated.

But the time came when she had to contact Lee about the Labor Day parade and the visit to the children's hospital which was scheduled for the same day. She worked herself into a nervous state over calling him, but when she finally did, she was surprised at her reception. He was pleasant and professional, acting as if nothing had happened between them. She felt as if she were in a time warp, and had somehow been transported back to the days of their initial acquaintance. She was relieved, and yet perversely disappointed, that he'd apparently forgotten the incident.

However, when Lee's schedule arrived in her office and Mr. Salamone called her and asked her to deliver it personally to Lee that day, her newly restored calm disappeared.

4

~oooooooooo~

The ride to Lee's house was a stressful one for Jennifer. She did not like the idea of going to his home. It was somehow too intimate for the distance she was trying to maintain between them. But he had to have the material that day. There was no help for it. The guard at the security station recognized her and waved her on.

She pulled into the lot behind his condominium and got out of the car, scanning the numbers as she walked. Each had a fenced yard, and she found Lee outside his house, in the middle of a workout.

He was so absorbed that he did not see her. She stopped, fascinated. She couldn't tear her eyes away from the sight of him, naked to the waist, clad only in brief cut-off denims and sneakers, going through his exercises. The sun gleamed on his bronze skin, giving it a soft luster, and his jet hair, mussed from exertion, clung to his head with dampness.

He paused for a moment, hands on hips, to catch his breath, still unaware of her presence. Jennifer stood behind the fence, knowing that she should speak and let him see that she was there, but spellbound by this glimpse of his dedication to his craft. He always acted as if his lightning speed and miraculous coordination were gifts of nature, which to a great extent they were, but this punishing daily routine was part of the package, too. He had to work hard to stay in the peak of physical condition, and she felt foolish for not realizing it before this. Perhaps it was because of her experience with Bob, who should have had Lee's dedication but never did and, consequently, was plagued by injuries and illness.

Lee bent to wipe his face with a towel draped over the handlebars of an exercise bike standing nearby. Perspiration ran in rivulets on his arms and streamed down his chest and heavily muscled abdomen. The waistband of his shorts was soaked.

Jennifer took the opportunity to knock. She rapped on the gate, calling, "Lee. It's Jennifer. I have the itinerary for the parade."

He looked up, pushing back his hair, and took a gray T-shirt from the seat of the bike, pulling it over his head as he came toward her. She felt a little better with him covered up, but not much. His physical presence was still overwhelming.

"Hi," he said, unlatching the gate and stepping aside to let her pass. "Come on inside. It's broiling out here."

Jennifer followed him gratefully through the sliding glass doors by the patio into air-conditioned coolness. The interior was furnished as a bachelor pad, with lots of deep, leather furniture and rustic wood. A sleek ultramodern galley kitchen of copper and stainless steel opened into a large dining area fronting the patio. Beyond, there was a sunken living room with a huge fieldstone fireplace, twin loveseats in taupe suede flanking it, and a floor to ceiling, well-stocked bar. Above she could see an overhanging balcony and loft, which obviously led to the bedrooms. The floor in the kitchen and hall was of brick-red quarry tiles. The rest of the rooms were carpeted in eggshell wool, thick, luxurious. The total effect was chic, tasteful, and expensive.

"This is very nice," she said coolly, trying not to show how impressed she was.

He looked around. "Thanks," he said vaguely. "I bought it for when I'm in town, but I won't be using it much. I'm on the road with the team most of the season."

Quite an elaborate arrangement for a place he would hardly use. Well, he had the money to throw around if he wanted to buy a home in every major city.

"I was working out when you arrived," he said, "and I'm afraid I'm not fit company for a lady right now. Would you mind if I took a quick shower?"

That conjured up mental images Jennifer did not wish to consider. "Of course not. Go ahead."

"May I get you anything before I go? A drink? Iced tea?"

Such exaggerated politeness, coming from him, almost struck her funny. He was going out of his way to be deferential, and she found herself wondering why. Then she dismissed it. There was no reason to be suspicious.

"No, thank you. I'm fine."

"I'll be back shortly," he said and vanished up the stairs.

Jennifer occupied herself in his absence by examining the knickknacks and photos in the room. There were several framed shots of Youngson receiving awards and a group portrait of what was obviously his family. Lee resembled his father, a handsome, middle-aged man who wore the same speculative expression she had often seen on Lee's face.

Two studies on the polished oak mantel of the
fireplace particularly caught her eye. One was an
8 x 10 glossy of a younger, more innocent Lee,
grinning openly into the camera, holding a trophy
and standing next to a man in a business suit who
was shaking his hand.

The other was of Lee and a beautiful young girl
with long black hair and a proud, unflinching gaze.
He had his arm around her possessively. They were
both in fancy dress, Lee in a tuxedo, the girl in a
gown of a style popular ten or twelve years ago.

Jennifer was examining the second picture when
she heard Lee behind her on the stairs. She moved
away guiltily.

Lee had changed into white duck pants with a
narrow belt and a short-sleeved sport shirt of crisp,
light cotton. The outfit was oddly 1920s, like something out of The Great Gatsby. His primitive good
looks meshed effectively with the WASPish clothes.

He had hurried to return: his hair was still wet, and
damp patches on his skin made the thin material of
his shirt cling to his body. There was a faint splotch of
white powder on the side of his throat.

Jennifer looked away.

Lee came and sat beside her, and the clean scent
of soap wafted from him as he did so. She moved
back, very slightly. He noticed it and glanced at her.
She could not tell what he was thinking.

Jennifer carefully went over the schedule of events
in which he was to participate. He listened attentive-
ly, asked pertinent questions, and their business was
accomplished in less than an hour.

Jennifer gathered her notes and rose. He stood,
too, seemingly reluctant to end the interview.

"Thanks for coming out here," he said. "It was

kind of you to let me know the rundown as soon as you got it."

Jennifer moved to leave and was startled when he detained her with his hand on her arm.

She looked up at him. He remained with his fingers clasping her wrist.

"Will you have dinner with me Saturday night?" he said suddenly.

Jennifer stared at him, stunned. She had not expected this, after their last encounter.

He waited, his face impassive.

Jennifer didn't know what to say. Did she want to go? Was the sky blue? But this man unsettled her; he was so out of the common way, so new to her experience, that he was at once fascinating and unnerving. She had no idea what to expect from a social evening with him. Except that it wouldn't be dull.

"I . . . I think I'd like that," she heard herself say.

Lee's expression softened.

"Great. I'll call you, then?"

"Fine," Jennifer said, escaping.

She drove back to the office in a daze, unable to believe that she had a date with the National Football League's Most Valuable Player three years in a row, the Cawassa Comet, the Blackfoot Bullet, Bradley Beaufort Youngson.

Jennifer changed three times for her dinner with Lee Youngson. He had telephoned on Thursday, asking if Chez Odette would be all right and saying that he would pick her up at eight.

Chez Odette was a fancy French restaurant on the outskirts of New Hope, very atmospheric, with a picturesque setting on the barge canal of the Dela-

ware River. She didn't have much that was suitable
to wear to such a place, and she tortured herself with
various combinations of clothes, jewelry, shoes, and
handbags, until in desperation she went back to her
first idea and settled on that.

She waited nervously for him to arrive, dressed in
a pale blue linen suit with a sheer blouse designed to
reveal a delicate, lacy camisole beneath. Milky pearls
gleamed at her ears and in the hollow of her throat.
She had teamed high-heeled pumps with a leather
clutch bag and sprayed herself with her most expensive perfume. She was ready.

Jennifer listened for the low hum of Lee's sports
car, checking herself in the mirror again, patting her
hair. It hung loose and shining to her shoulders. Her
lipstick was fresh and her eye shadow properly
muted.

She looked at her watch. It was 7:45.

She spent twelve agonizing minutes thinking
about everything that could go wrong until the
doorbell rang at three minutes to eight. She'd been
so absorbed in her contemplation of doom that she
hadn't heard the car after all.

Jennifer opened the door, and they looked at each
other. Lee was wearing a nubbly raw silk jacket, the
color of sand, obviously tailor-made, that empha-
sized his imposing physique. The off-white shirt and
figured tie perfectly complemented his coat and the
brown, well-cut slacks. She recognized Gucci loafers.
No expense spared when escorting Ms. Gardiner.

His eyes moved from Jennifer's face, down her
body, and then back to her face again. "You look
lovely," he said softly.

So do you, Jennifer thought, as he guided her
down the path to his car and handed her into the

passenger seat. She noticed again that fine apparel only seemed to underline his aspect of brooding, primal strength. Just below the surface was the magnificent leashed animal, latent, powerful. The window dressing only served to make him more of what he was. The effect was dynamite.

I'll bet he knows it, too, Jennifer mused as she settled back for the ride. I have to keep my cool, she thought again. Whatever had made him ask her out and renew their relationship, she mustn't read too much into it.

The drive to the restaurant was wonderful, cool and breezy, laden with the fragrance of late summer flowers. Lee asked her if she wanted him to leave the top down, and she said yes, thinking that she could repair whatever damage occurred when they got to the restaurant. The glorious feel of the wind in her hair was worth it. He offered her the choice of his collection of tapes, and she examined the stack. He had a collection of classical pieces, for which she wasn't in the mood, and some jazz, which she didn't like. At the bottom she found several vintage rock 'n' roll albums. She selected Buddy Holly, and the familiar sounds of "Peggy Sue" and "Not Fade Away" floated into the evening air.

They knew Lee Youngson at Chez Odette. Waiters came running from all directions when they entered, and the maître d' was obsequious. The main dining room was crowded, but they were shown immediately to the best table, out of the traffic pattern, with a view of the gardens below them. Jennifer wondered who Lee's companions had been on his previous visits.

She glanced around her as they were seated. The whole restaurant was furnished in gold and white

French provincial, with creamy damask tablecloths
and patterned linen napkins at each table. There was
a large vase of fresh flowers, roses and carnations, in
the center of theirs, which complemented the color
of the shell pink, delicate china and the heavy,
gleaming silver. Chez Odette was rich in atmosphere.
She was sure the patrons paid for it.

Jennifer excused herself to go to the powder room
and tidy her hair. Heads turned as she passed, and
she heard the murmur of muted comments. Lee's
date was a source of interest.

When she returned, she found that Lee had
ordered wine, but there was only one glass, at her
place. He stood to seat her, and she asked why he
wasn't having any.

"What's the matter with you, Jennifer? You know
Indians aren't supposed to drink. Can't handle
demon firewater. Don't you watch old movies?"

Her eyes flashed to his face. When he made a
remark like this, she still didn't know whether he was
kidding or not.

He met her gaze intently for a moment, and then
smiled slightly. "Relax, paleface. I'm in training. You
go ahead, though."

Jennifer sipped sparingly. She had no intention of
getting giddy while he sat there observing her sober-
ly. And she wasn't sure she cared for his calling her
"paleface." There was an edge to his voice when he
said it tonight that she didn't like.

"You stick to the rules, don't you?" she said
pleasantly. "Daily workouts, no tobacco, no booze,
no drugs." Bob hadn't had the same reverence for
his body. His drunken bouts, and the fines which
followed, had given him a reputation as a bad risk.

"It's made me what I am today," Lee said cynically.

"There's no need to be snide," Jennifer responded. "I meant it as a compliment." She couldn't understand his behavior. It was almost as if he wanted to punish her for the time of silence following the Heart Fund game. Was that the reason for this dinner invitation?

"Did you?" he said. "That's a first."

Why was he doing this? "I think your dedication is admirable," she added, trying to smooth the waters.

He raised his water glass in a mock toast. "Coming from a paragon of self-discipline like you, that's high praise indeed."

"If you asked me out only because you wanted to needle me, you're wasting your money. You could have done that on the job, where I would have been more disposed to tolerate it," Jennifer said quietly. "This is not my idea of a good time."

He dropped his eyes, avoiding looking at her for a moment. Then his brown hand covered hers on the immaculate tablecloth.

"Nor mine either," he said softly. "I'm sorry, Jennifer."

The touch of his slender fingers was electric, the sound of her name on his lips more intoxicating then the wine she was drinking. This one was a shaman, like his great-grandfather, weaving spells to break your heart.

"Harold told me that your ex-husband was an athlete," he said unexpectedly.

"Yes." And here I am with you, Jennifer thought. Still running true to type.

"Football?" he asked, not letting the subject drop.

"Baseball. Bob Delaney. He used to play for the Phillies; he's with the Chicago White Sox now."

Lee nodded. "I know him. Very talented, but very wild. If he ever learns to control himself enough to develop, he could be really great."

Jennifer smiled sadly. "He never will," she said. She had to admire Lee's perception. He had described Bob more accurately than she could have, and she had lived with Bob for years.

"Well," Lee said, seeing her reflective expression, "Satchel Paige once said something that could be applied to thoughts about the past. 'Don't look back, something may be gaining on you.'" He paused. "In my case it's usually true," he added ruefully.

She knew that he was referring to his performance in football games. Despite the fact that she had been working for the team for a while, she still didn't know much about the actual sport. From what she'd seen, Lee's part in it seemed to be limited to dramatic leaps to snatch the ball out of the air, followed by headlong flight down the field, the ball tucked under his arm, with opposing players pummeling after him in mad pursuit, trying to catch him. Few did. He ran, as Coach Rankin said, like a quarterback's dream, like a gazelle with a tiger on its tail.

Jennifer looked up from her reverie to see the waiter hovering at Lee's elbow. "Shall we order?" she said brightly.

The menu was in French on one side and in English on the other. Jennifer asked Lee to choose for her. He ordered the same for both: escargots in garlic butter, pâté de foie gras, chateaubriand, and a vinaigrette of vegetables.

Everything was delicious. The waiters served sherbet and lemon wedges between each course, to "cleanse the palate," and brought hot, moist cloths scented with mint to wash their hands at the end. Musicians strolled about the room, the violinist stopping for a solo at several tables. Jennifer was enchanted.

Lee suggested a walk outside before coffee and dessert. He said something to the waiter, and they left through the double doors, pausing once for Lee to sign a napkin for a fan who had recognized him.

"I like this place," he said to Jennifer as they descended the wide stone steps to the garden below. "They leave me alone here. In some restaurants, I can't even eat, I'm so mobbed by autograph seekers."

"The price of fame," Jennifer said dryly. "Of course, if they all lost interest in you and stopped buying tickets, you'd be out of a job. But you'd be able to dine anywhere in peace."

He stopped short, looking down at her in the dim light from the lanterns on the footpath. "I guess I deserved that You're right." He shook his head. "You certainly speak your mind, don't you? I've tried that line on a few other girls, and they all murmured in deep sympathy."

Jennifer smiled. "My father, who loves me, refers to my bluntness as 'refreshing candor.' My stepmother, who doesn't, calls it 'bad manners.'"

Lee chuckled. "I prefer 'refreshing candor,' myself." He took her hand and led her to a fountain in the midst of enclosing greenery. There was a wrought-iron bench there, surrounded by masses of brilliant geraniums and zinnias. They sat.

"This is beautiful," Jennifer said. She pointed to the lush stand of maples and oaks along the river bank. "How pretty the trees are, so full."

"Yeah," Lee sighed, following the direction of her gaze. "It kind of makes you realize what this country must have been like before progress ruined it." He picked a scarlet blossom from a bush behind them and handed it to her. "There's a poem by Ogden Nash that, for me, sums it up." He recited the verse.

Jennifer burst out laughing, and he grinned, pleased with himself. His teeth shone very white in the semidarkness.

"Think I'm a funny guy?" he said, teasing.

"I think you're a . . . nice guy," Jennifer said softly, before she could stop herself. "Even though you try to hide it."

He turned to her abruptly and took her in his arms. Her head dropped to his shoulder, and he kissed her.

His lips were soft, a contrast to his hard, spare frame. The kiss began as a leisurely exploration, but soon escalated until Jennifer was clinging to him, the only stable object in a spinning universe. His hands dug into her shoulders, holding her fast against his body. She heard a noise as another couple passed them, and she broke away, startled and ashamed. She hadn't necked in public since high school.

Lee didn't seem to be bothered by the interruption. "I've missed you, Jennifer, these past few weeks," he whispered, caressing her hair.

"We'd better go in," Jennifer said. "They're holding dessert for us."

"Let them wait," he said urgently, pulling her back against his chest.

"No," Jennifer insisted, resisting him, struggling to her feet. She was frightened by the depth of her response to him. Not since Bob . . . no, she had to be honest with herself. Not even Bob had made her feel like this. It was like the Heart Fund picnic all over again.

"I want to go back," she said unsteadily.

Lee followed her reluctantly, then trotted up the steps to hold the door for her.

The minute they arrived back at the table a silver pot of coffee appeared, and a busboy brought a dessert cart filled with delicate pastries. Jennifer selected two exquisite petits fours iced with pastel fondant and a miniature éclair. Lee shook his head, and the cart was rolled away.

The coffee was Indonesian, rich and aromatic. They drank it in silence, the passionate interlude in the garden not forgotten.

By the time Lee signed the check and called for his car, Jennifer had become tongue-tied again. From the encouragement she'd given him he would probably press his advantage when he brought her home, and she was not sure she could resist him. She had no desire to become another trophy to hang on his wall, but she wanted him. Badly. His very touch set her off like a match put to kindling. If he tried, it would not be easy to say no.

The drive back to her apartment was a quiet one, interrupted only by Lee's comments on the scenery, and the click of the tape deck as it switched from the Everly Brothers to Jerry Lee Lewis. Lee's long fingers tapped the steering wheel as he drove. Jennifer glanced across at him, and he caught her eye and smiled. She looked away again, her heart beating faster. He communicated without words, with an almost physical impact. She felt kissed, by a smile.

When they turned onto Main Street and Dr. Mason's house came into view, every nerve in

Jennifer's body tightened. Lee pulled into the driveway, turned off the motor, and got out to open her door. Jennifer emerged from the passenger side, and he stood in front of her, blocking her path. Her nose came to his collarbone.

He put one hand on her shoulder and tipped her chin up wtih the forefinger of the other. "Aren't you going to invite me in?"

"I . . . don't think that would be a good idea." She fumbled in her purse for her keys.

"Please, Jennifer. Just for a minute. Please."

She found her keys and he took them from her. She followed him upstairs, telling herself that she had to be firm. When he opened her door and ushered her into her apartment, she decided that she'd just make him coffee and then firmly send him home.

She went directly to the stove and put water on to boil.

"Would you like coffee, or would you prefer a drink?" she said, trying to keep her words even.

He didn't answer.

Jennifer pulled cups and saucers out of the cabinet above, and then turned back to the room, directly into Lee's arms. He held her for a moment, not saying anything, and she inhaled the heady fragrance of him, the starch of his shirt, the flax of his coat, the subtle warmth of his skin. Then his touch on her neck moved her face to his, and his lips found hers again.

His mouth clung to hers with a fierceness that robbed her of breath. Her breasts were crushed against his chest by the force of one powerful hand splayed in the small of her back. She responded, helpless, and his lips moved to her cheek, her ear, and traveled down her throat. With one impatient gesture he removed her suit jacket.

His eyes devoured her, and then with a small sound deep in his throat he embraced her again. His hands sank into her thick hair, running the gossamer strands through his fingers, as if he loved the feel of it. With one arm across her he turned her back to him and fitted himself against her. She whimpered at the intimate contact. He drew her hair back and mouthed the nape of her neck, his hands moving up from her waist to enclose her breasts, sheathed only by the flimsy camisole.

"Where's the bedroom?" he said, his voice low and husky in her ear.

His words brought her back to reality. She was one step away from an irrevocable act, and she panicked. He was holding her loosely, ready to move, and she slipped out of his grasp.

She faced him, her skin burning, knowing that she had teased him unfairly, without meaning to. "I can't," she said.

He stared at her, breathing hard, hands on hips, much as she had seen him the day she found him exercising. But there was another reason for his breathlessness now. She looked at him, so handsome, so desirable. . . . And more than that. He was courageous, sensitive, witty . . . Stop it! she instructed herself. I will not become involved with another athlete. Remember the last time, the hurt, the pain? The endless road trips, the losing streaks, the injuries, the groupies? Oh, no, don't do it again.

"Why not?" he asked, agonized.

"I just can't do it," she said, realizing how unsatisfactory an answer that was, but unable to explain to him that she was afraid to let him get too close to her, that she didn't want to be hurt again, that she thought he would have the power to hurt her even more than Bob Delaney.

He saw her struggle, and held up his hand. "Forget it. If the answer is no, it's no. I won't bother you again."

I believe you, Jennifer thought miserably.

Her extreme unhappiness must have shown in her face, because his look suddenly softened. He almost smiled.

"Don't look so tragic, paleface. Believe it or not, it's not the first time I've been turned down. I think I'll survive it."

"I had a lovely time," she said in a small voice.

His mouth twisted "Ever the soul of graciousness," he responded. "I think if you were about to be executed you'd be thanking the headsman for the use of his ax." He inclined his head slightly. "Good night."

Jennifer met his eyes quickly and then looked away. "Good night."

She heard the sound of his footsteps on the stairs, followed by the roar of the car's motor. Then all was silence.

The kettle began to whistle. She automatically shut it off, feeling more alone than she had for a long time.

5

~~~~~~~~~~~

Weeks passed, during which Jennifer kept herself busy. This was not difficult, considering the volume of work she had to complete before the season began. When Lee did come into her mind, she dismissed him abruptly, refusing to entertain disturbing thoughts.

But she knew she would have to deal with her feelings on Labor Day, when she would see him again. His presence always brought everything she was trying to bury to the surface, so she began constructing an elaborate defense several days before they would have to meet. She would be polite, but distant. She would be friendly, but reserved. There was nothing to worry about; it was very simple. Right.

The holiday morning was warm and sunny, but without the crushing humidity Jennifer found so difficult to bear. She dressed in lightweight, dark blue slacks and a nautical top with a square collar and tie bib. When the limousine arrived to get her, her palms were wet and her mouth was dry. Calm down, she advised herself sternly, annoyed with her inability to control her autonomic responses.

When they got to Lee's house, he was not outside, ready, as he had been the last time. Jennifer told the driver to wait and went up the steps to ring the bell.

Lee's voice hailed her from the depths of the house, telling her to come in, the door was open.

Jennifer found him in the kitchen, leaning against the stainless steel sink, legs crossed at the ankles. He was sipping coffee from an earthenware mug. Bruce Springsteen sang throatily in the background.

"Hi," he said. "Want some coffee? According to the timetable which management so thoughtfully provided, we've got a few minutes." He gestured to another mug sitting on the counter.

His ability to dismiss their previous encounters and start afresh left her at a loss. Didn't he remember what had happened the last time they saw each other? Jennifer certainly did.

But he regarded her impassively over the rim of the cup. "My instructions were to dress casually," he added. He jerked a thumb at himself. "This is it."

He was wearing white jeans and a blood red shirt. Jennifer had always envied people who were able to wear scarlet and carry it off. The same shade dulled Jennifer's hair to insignificance and drained her skin to chalk white. His striking hair and eyes were needed to complement it. In that color, most people would look three days dead.

"Joined the navy?" he asked, indicating her outfit, smiling slightly.

Jennifer picked up the other mug and filled it from the pot on the stove. "Joined the palace guard?" she countered, pointing to his shirt.

He choked on his coffee, sputtering with laughter. He set the cup down and shook his head, regarding her with a grin. "Touché. You give back as good as you get, every time."

She smiled back at him, caught in the spell once again. "Part of my charm," she said negligently.

He sobered, watching her. "Yes, it is," he said quietly.

Jennifer dropped her eyes, unsure of how to respond. He frequently turned the tables on her like this. Just when she was sure she was on safe ground, bantering, where she could hold her own with anybody, he would suddenly turn serious and leave her nonplussed. It made conversation with him a constant challenge.

"Want some cream?" he asked, going to the refrigerator.

"Thanks."

He took a fresh pint from a shelf and pried the cap off with his teeth.

"Good heavens, Lee, your dentist would have a heart attack if he saw that," she said.

"Nah," he answered, adding a dollop to her cup, "these Indian choppers are indestructible. They may not be perfectly straight, we didn't go in much for orthodontics on the reservation, but they're strong as iron." He cast her a sidelong glance. "Comes from chowing buffalo hides."

He was teasing, as usual. "I may not be that well versed in the practices of your culture," Jennifer said archly, "but even I know that only women did that work."

Lee shrugged. "That was before the ERA hit the tribe. Now we all do it."

Jennifer kept a straight face. "Sounds like a sensible plan."

His eyes twinkled. "Actually, the Blackfeet were always a pretty liberated bunch. The teepee belonged to the wife, you know, and if she and her husband had a fight, she could throw him out and leave him homeless."

"I'll drink to that," Jennifer said, and did so.

"And," Lee went on, "the wife kept her maiden name all her life. She was not regarded as her husband's property, but his partner."

Jennifer set down her cup and applauded.

He grinned. "I thought you'd like that."

Jennifer looked at her watch. "Don't you think we'd better get started?"

"Yes, ma'am," he responded, putting the cups in the sink. He walked around and switched off the stereo just as the record was going into the title cut, "Born to Run."

"My theme song," Lee said. He looked back at her. "In more ways than one."

What exactly did that mean? He was talking on two levels, and Jennifer had a suspicion that the hidden meaning had something to do with her.

As they walked into the hall she pointed to one of the photographs on the mantelpiece. "Is that your father?"

Lee nodded.

"He must be very proud of you."

Lee's eyes became distant, focused elsewhere. "Yes, he is. I think he's living his life over again, through me. The reservation ruined him, took away his ambition, initiative, everything. He wanted to see that the same thing didn't happen to me, so when sports gave me the chance to break free of that life, he made sure I took it."

Jennifer was silent.

"Of course," Lee continued, "getting off the reservation isn't always the answer. Take my sister. Please."

Jennifer waited for what was to come. The old joke was stated in a bitter tone that signified more.

"Her name," Lee said, "is Spring Flower, except now she's changed it to 'Fleur.' She says it sounds more sophisticated, but what she really means is that it sounds French, which is okay, as opposed to Indian, which is not."

His voice was filled with rancor. "She won a scholarship to college, like me, except once she got there she forgot where she came from. She hasn't been back to see my parents in six years."

Jennifer didn't know what to say.

"She's a research chemist for some big laboratory in New Jersey. It's not that far from here, actually, but I haven't been able to bring myself to go see her. She acts like she has no past, that her life began at eighteen when she left home. I'm sure none of the people she works with know about her background. She's careful to conceal it. That doesn't explain her looks, though, so I understand the guy she's engaged to tells everybody that her mother is Greek."

Jennifer couldn't imagine why he was telling her all this. Her innocent question about the picture had prompted this outpouring of personal information.

"Well," Lee added, "I'm sure they'll be very happy. The only successful marriages I've ever seen between Indians and non-Indians occur when the Indian is totally absorbed in WASP culture. And my sister is well on her way to becoming an imitation WASP. Something," he said with precision, "that I will never be."

Jennifer was sure of that. If the transformation hadn't occurred by now, it never would.

"Your sister doesn't mean to hurt anyone, Lee," Jennifer said soothingly. "She's probably just confused."

"I'm not," Lee said firmly. "I don't know how

people can just dismiss their heritage like that, no matter what it could gain them or how much they loved someone. I could never do it."

Jennifer felt a chill. Was he trying to tell her something? But his expression was abstracted, as if he had forgotten she was there and he were talking to himself.

"Surely it doesn't always have to be like that," Jennifer said softly, "with one person selling out for the other. I'm certain that sometimes both people can accept what they are and love each other while still keeping their identities intact."

"I've never seen it," Lee answered.

Jennifer had nothing to add to that. After all, he was in a position to know.

He turned his head and seemed to remember the reason for her presence.

"Let's go, counselor," he said, sighing. "Our chariot awaits."

The parade route began at the Museum of Art and traveled through downtown Philadelphia, winding up at Independence Hall. Lee rode a float with several other athletes, including Joe Thornridge, while Jennifer used the interim time to advantage talking to the newspaper and television people about Lee's visit to the children's hospital, scheduled for that afternoon. It was a great human interest story, and Jennifer planned to get a lot of mileage out of it.

After the parade there was a short press conference, and Jennifer waited for Lee in the background. She was looking over her notes when she felt a touch on her shoulder and jumped.

"Hi," Lee said.

She had been so absorbed that she hadn't realized he was already finished.

"Don't creep up on me like that," she said breathlessly. "How'd it go?"

"Fine. I waved at everybody and looked appropriately macho. The crowd seemed suitably impressed."

His tone was dry. Obviously, being on display was not his favorite thing.

"Well, you have a couple of hours before you're due at the hospital," Jennifer said. "The driver can take you home if you like."

"Are you going home, too?" he quizzed.

"I guess so. I have to change."

"All right. You can drop me off on the way." He folded his arms and surveyed the impressive facade of Independence Hall over her shoulder. She turned to follow his gaze, taking in the colonial brick structure with the gleaming white bell tower.

"Look at this place," he said. "You ever been inside?"

"I took the tour once, a while ago."

"The walls speak to you, don't they? You can almost imagine old Patrick Henry making that speech: 'Give me liberty, or give me death.' Great stuff. Them's fightin' words. Quite a phrase to echo down through the generations. You have to admire those people. They risked everything, and I mean everything, for what they thought was right. I remember some history teacher talking about that comment John Hancock made when he signed the Declaration of Independence. You know, 'I'll write this big enough for King George to see without his glasses on.'"

"Yes, I remember."

"Well, this teacher said that people repeat it today as though it were a joke or something, but they forget that Hancock thought he might have been signing his death warrant. What courage that took. When I saw the original, preserved, the way they have it, there was John's signature, three times as large as the others, and I couldn't believe it. You hear about something all your life, and it becomes almost a myth, as though it doesn't really exist anywhere but in your mind. It was a kick to finally see the real thing."

Jennifer stared at him. Here he was expressing admiration for the colonial patriots, the forerunners of those who had eventually enslaved his people.

He saw her look, and knew its meaning. He shrugged. "Great Britain was wrong," he said. "It's my country, too," he added quietly. Then he cupped her chin in the palm of one large hand and turned her face up to his. "In fact, it was my country before it was yours."

That was certainly true. She locked eyes with him for a few seconds, and then stepped back, saying briskly, "I'll go inside and call Max to pick us up."

Lee leaned gracefully against a lamppost and said, "I'll be here."

As Jennifer walked away she thought about what he had said. Upon closer examination, his enthusiasm for the Founding Fathers was more understandable. She could see how their actions would appeal to his sense of style. He had a flair for the dramatic himself. She had seen him pause in the end zone after making a touchdown and hold the ball aloft, like a lady's favor in a joust, to the vocal delight of the fans. Then he would bend from the waist in a sweeping, courtly bow. She had thought at first that the other players might resent these histrionics, and think him a hot dog, but he really wasn't one, and they apparently knew it. In interviews, he never failed to give credit to his defense people, the blockers and tackles who cleared the way for his flashy footwork, and he always praised Joe Thornridge for his magic arm.

On the way back he was quiet and merely nodded when she reminded him of the time she would return for him. She watched him walk up the path to his house, admiring, as always, the broad shoulders and narrow waist, the perfect proportions of his athlete's body. The sun made a shining black helmet of his hair. Then she tore her eyes away and ordered Max, in a firmer tone than was necessary, to take her back to her apartment.

She told herself sternly that she really hadn't been hoping Lee would ask her inside.

They were due at the hospital at two, and Jennifer ate a quick lunch before changing into a tailored dress and brushing her hair. She glanced at the evening dress laid out on the bed for the dinner that night. Sponsored by the Freedom's management, it was being held at the Bellevue Stratford downtown, to welcome the new players and kick off the season. It was a social event, rather than business, so she wouldn't be going with Lee. For lack of a better idea, she had asked John Ashford to escort her, and she assumed Lee was bringing a date also.

Jennifer shook her head. One thing at a time. She had to get through this afternoon first. She would worry about tonight when the time came.

Lee remained introspective during the ride to the

hospital. He sat next to her in the back seat of the
limousine, his knee almost touching hers, staring out
the window. He had changed also, into dark slacks
and a light blue shirt and a knit tie. He turned once to
find her watching him, and she looked away.

A group of reporters and a news team from a local
television station were already waiting outside the
ward when they arrived. A cameraman with his
equipment strapped to his shoulders zeroed in on
Lee and followed his every move. Lee glanced at
Jennifer quickly, uncertainly, as if for guidance, and
then plunged ahead.

The kids could hardly control their excitement.
The ambulatory cases had been assembled at one
end of the ward, where rows of folding chairs were
interspersed with wheelchairs and cots. The children
who were bedridden had been propped up with
pillows so they could see better. Nurses and aides
stood by, beaming, to shake hands with Lee as he
entered. A hospital spokesman, who had met them
in the lobby, cleared the way and led Lee to a
vantage point where he could address the group.

Lee's reaction to the sick children was not lost on
Jennifer. His sharp eyes took in everything, and they
filled with compassion at the sight of illness and
incapacity in ones so young. He paused a couple of
times, once by the bedside of a little black boy who
had tubes running from his nose and the inside of his
arm. He sat on the edge of the child's bed, as
everyone waited for him, and talked to the boy for
several minutes. He stopped again to tell a girl of
about nine or ten, who had a broken leg in traction,
about the time he had broken his own leg. He
reassured the girl that his was as good as new now,
and hers would be, too.

Jennifer walked just behind him, and she could see his face change during his progress through the ward. When he got to his appointed spot, he looked around for her.

"Jen?" he said softly.

She had never heard that tone from him before. He, who was always so sure of himself, sounded . . . shaken.

"Right here," she said, stepping forward.

He looked at her for a moment, and then reached down and pressed her hand.

Alarmed, she said, "Lee, are you all right?"

He swallowed. "Sure. Fine. Just . . . stay here, okay?"

In that moment, she would have done anything he asked. "I'll be right behind you."

He nodded. "Let's get this show on the road."

The photographers snapped pictures, and the reporters held up their microphones to catch his words, as he began a dialogue with the children, answering their questions and telling them stories. As he relaxed, and the effects of what had been bothering him initially wore off, he loosened his tie and pulled a chair forward to lean on as he talked.

His audience was fascinated. They listened, quiet as cloistered nuns, their eyes round, while he described the rigors of the Sun Dance, a solemn ceremony performed by the Indians of the Plains for hundreds of years. Jennifer was as riveted as the children by the narration. Lee told of the preparation involved, the feasting, the courtships, and the selection of the assistants for the rites by the shamans. Virtuous women were chosen to chop down the sacred cottonwood tree, used as an integral part of the dance. Later, a mentor would be chosen from the shamans to be in charge of the activities.

The cottonwood tree was then stripped, painted, and raised as a pole in the center of the dancing ground. At dawn, the dancers were prepared for their ordeal. The warriors were decorated with colors that showed what degree of pain they had chosen to suffer. Some would merely fast and dance, others would have bits of flesh cut from their bodies, and the bravest were those who had agreed to have skewers implanted through flaps cut in their skin. They were attached to the tree, or to buffalo skulls, by rawhide thongs, and would dance until the skin of each man ripped free from the skewers, experiencing, through their great pain, a communion with the spirit of the sun.

Jennifer watched the children's expressions as Lee detailed, vividly, the endurance of the dancers, the trancelike state of the participants as they approached union with their god. It was clear that this group had never heard anything like it. She hadn't, either.

One child, bolder than the others, began to beg for a demonstration. Jennifer could tell that Lee was tempted, but he glanced at the reporters crowding around him, and it was obvious that he didn't want to be filmed for presentation on the six o'clock news. The spokesman had acquired a following, and Lee shushed them with the promise of another story. Jennifer watched, overwhelmed with tenderness, as Lee lost the last of his reserve and sat cross-legged on the floor, telling the children about the Blackfoot societies, through which the men of the tribe advanced all their lives. As boys they entered the Little Birds, where they learned the art of warfare. After three trials, a boy went on to the Pigeons, and when he was finally accepted as a warrior, to the Mosquitoes. He gave the Pikuni name for all of these. And, Lee said, if a man had the largest number of coups in his society, and had become a living god, then he could join the Mutsik, the society reserved for the bravest and best warriors. Lee's grandfather, Spotted Horse, had been a Mutsik, Lee told them proudly, and a great chief.

"What are coups?" a towheaded midget in the front row asked in a piping voice.

Lee explained that coups were blows delivered to the enemy by touching him with a coup stick. It was like a game of tag, he said, but a dangerous one, in which you had to get close enough to an armed enemy to touch him, but had to get away again to tell the story. The tribal council then listened to the story of the deed, and if it was determined to be the truth, supported by witnesses, the brave was awarded a coup feather, a tail feather of the male golden eagle. The warrior collected these, and when he had enough, he wore them in a warbonnet.

By this time, the reporters had material for their stories, and the nurses were making noises about getting the children back to bed. When it was time for Lee to go, amidst much protest, the redhead who had talked the most touched Lee on the arm and said wistfully, "Sure wish we could have seen that dance."

The members of the press were gone, and Lee said good-bye to the staff, promising to return. He pushed his hair back from his forehead and exhaled sharply.

"Do you think you could go along without me?" he asked Jennifer. "I'm through here, but I want to talk to the administrator about some fund raiser they want me to do. I don't want to hold you up, so you might as well go home. I'll call a cab."

This was another breach of the rules, but she wasn't about to debate it with him. "All right, Lee. You look tired, though; you'd better get out of here early enough to get some rest before tonight. By the way, what was upsetting you when you first came in?"

His eyes flashed to her face. "Oh, nothing."

"Something, I think."

He sighed. "It was just, well, I had a brother who died of leukemia when he was eleven, and this sort of brought it all back to me. I had forgotten how . . . painful . . . it is to see sick children and not be able to help them."

Jennifer was silent.

"I did want to help them, once. I wanted to be a doctor. Did I ever tell you that?"

"I think you mentioned it, yes."

He nodded slowly. "All water under the bridge, now, I guess." He eyed her, his head slightly tilted to one side. "I'll see you tonight, then."

"Yes."

His lips curved in the trace of a smile. "Thanks for the moral support."

"That's my job," she said lightly, and then was sorry for the superficial comment. His expression changed.

"Ah, yes, the job. You *are* very good at your job."

The closeness between them had vanished in an instant. Jennifer lifted her hand in farewell and headed out to the parking lot, as Lee turned away.

She was almost to the glass double doors at the end of the hall when something made her stop. Lee's behavior had been abrupt, suspect in a vague way, as if he had wanted to be rid of her. The story about the fund raiser had sounded hastily manufactured. What was he up to? Jennifer turned around and retraced her steps.

Her suspicions were confirmed when she got back to the ward. Two nurses stood by the doors, like sentinels, blocking entry. They recognized Jennifer as Lee's companion and let her pass.

Lee was in the middle of the room, barefoot and bare chested, his shirt and shoes discarded on a nearby chair. Jennifer remained hidden behind an examination screen as Lee selected the redhead and two others to follow him as he demonstrated the Sun Dance. Gracefully, without a wasted motion, he showed the children the ancient, time-honored movements, pacing slowly in a circle, chanting softly under his breath. The kids, two boys and a little girl, mimed his every gesture, carefully, solemnly, as if their lives depended on getting it right. Lee looked like nothing so much as Pied Piper, his charges trailing after him in intricate procession.

Jennifer bit her lip and closed her eyes, smitten completely. How sweet he was to do this. He had come back on his own, without an audience, so as not to disappoint the kids.

When she looked again he was beating out the rhythm on one of the bedsteads, watching the children as they continued without him. Jennifer saw the bent dark head, the softly falling hands, and knew that she was in love with him.

It was not so bad once she found the courage to admit it to herself. She knew that nothing could ever come of it, he had made that eminently clear that morning, but acknowledging it gave her a secret treasure to hold next to her heart. She loved Lee Youngson, probably had since the day she'd met him. And just for that moment, before she could consider the heartbreak and the pain that would surely follow, she was glad.

She put her finger to her lips to indicate that she wished to remain undetected, and one of the nurses nodded as she slipped out again. The other followed her into the corridor.

"That is one very nice man," the nurse said to Jennifer.

"Yes, he is," Jennifer agreed.

"Those kids will be talking about this for weeks," her companion went on. "Just think, a famous person like that taking the time for them. It's made my day, I can tell you."

Jennifer exchanged a few more pleasantries with the woman and then left. During the ride home she kept seeing Lee dancing with those children, an image she couldn't, or wouldn't, dismiss from her mind.

Jennifer was determined to look her best that night. She might not be Lee's date, but she would see him and longed to make a lasting impression. After their dinner date she was sure that he wanted her; this gave her a heady feeling of power which she couldn't resist using. She deliberately chose her sexiest dress, a black off-the-shoulder taffeta with a scalloped hemline and puffed sleeves. She piled her hair on top of her head, adding earrings and a matching pendant of brilliant oval aquamarines surrounded by tiny diamonds. The jewelry was an anniversary present from Bob, which he, in a rare burst of chivalry, had refused to take back when they were divorced. The center stones enhanced her eyes, and the severe dress made her hair seem paler by contrast. When she was ready, she studied her reflection in the mirror and was sure that she had never looked better in her life.

Lee thought so, too. As she walked into the main dining room of the Bellevue Stratford with John Ashford, she saw Lee standing to one side with Joe Thornridge. Lee was resplendent in a white dinner jacket with satin lapels, a ruffled silk shirt, and narrow black pants with a black bowtie. His eyes traveled over Jennifer slowly and then met hers. In them, she saw a reflection of her own desire. Her breath caught in her throat, but she merely inclined her head coolly to acknowledge him. Lee did nothing, simply looked back at her with those searching, fathomless eyes. Jennifer turned her head and moved on.

Dolores was waiting at their table, with her date, a commercial photographer whom Jennifer had once met briefly. After she and John were seated, she looked around for Lee.

She had hoped that he would be placed out of her sight, but found to her dismay that he was only two tables away, with Joe Thornridge and his wife, a delicate blonde in a pastel pink dress. She had a clear view of Lee's chiseled profile and gleaming hair. And, unfortunately, an equally clear view of his date.

Jennifer really tried not to look, but found this impossible. She kept sneaking glances at the young woman, who was seated at Lee's left. She seemed familiar, and then Jennifer realized, with a start, that this was the same girl pictured with Lee in the photograph in his living room.

Jennifer examined her again, a few minutes later, and changed her mind. It wasn't the same person.

This one was a slightly distorted reflection in a mirror, like, and at the same time not like, the original in the photo. The cascading, waist-length black hair was the same, but this girl was slightly heavier, with a broader face and blunter features than the first. She was very pretty, but she was not the girl in the picture.

But then, who was she? There was a strong family resemblance—she had to be a relative of the girl in the photo, the likeness was too close. Jennifer burned with curiosity, and something like despair. Whoever she was, she was Indian, and Jennifer wasn't.

Harold Salamone got up on the dais to welcome the new players and wish the rest of the organization a prosperous year. Jennifer had heard it all before and studied her surroundings while the owner made his speech. The grand ballroom was huge, with an overhanging balcony surrounding the entire room, which was carpeted in red plush and dominated by a magnificent chandelier suspended from the ceiling by a golden chain. Salamone was talking from the stage, which had been converted to a speaker's platform for the executives. The rest of the organization was seated at banquet tables scattered about on the ballroom floor. A large central area had been left clear for dancing, and a small orchestra was setting up in the pit below the stage. Waiters roved through the throng, taking drink orders and carrying silver buckets of champagne and other wines. It was a glittering, picturesque group, and Jennifer felt privileged to be part of it.

After Salamone, a few others spoke, and then the music began as dinner was served. Jennifer ate sparingly, her stomach in a knot, ever mindful of the man two tables away, as if the two of them were alone in the room.

The band played between courses, and Jennifer danced with John and with Dolores's escort, Craig Davenport. Just before dessert she went to the powder room and on the way back ran straight into Lee and his date as they came off the dance floor.

There was no avoiding an introduction. Lee, ever the gentleman, presented the women to one another. His companion was Dawn Blacktree.

Harold Salamone came up to talk to Lee as they stood there, and Jennifer was left to converse with Dawn alone. She learned that Dawn was indeed the sister of the young woman in the picture at Lee's house. The latter had been Lee's high school sweetheart, until she was killed in a fall from a horse when she was seventeen.

This information did not make Jennifer feel better. Lee's bond with this girl was sure to be very strong. And to make matters worse, she couldn't even dislike Dawn, who was friendly and pleasant.

Joe Thornridge's wife came up to ask Dawn something, and Jennifer found herself in a three-way conversation with Lee and Harold Salamone. She smiled a lot and wished she were elsewhere. Finally, Mr. Salamone took his leave.

"May your time with us be very happy, and your career here a success," he said to Lee, grasping both of Lee's hands in his. Lee thanked him, his lips twitching, and put his hand over his mouth as the older man walked away.

It was a few seconds before Jennifer realized that Lee was laughing. His shoulders were shaking, and there was a wicked gleam in his dark eyes.

"What is it?" she said.

Lee coughed to cover his mirth. "I'm fond of Harold, I really am," he said, "but I can hardly keep a straight face when he talks to me. Everything he says sounds like the inscription on a greeting card."

This was so true that Jennifer found herself squelching laughter, too. Salamone was a master of banalities, and the more she thought about it, the funnier it became. She and Lee turned away from one another, unable to look at each other for fear of breaking up, like a couple of teen-agers overcome with forbidden hilarity in church.

Jennifer finally risked a glance at him, and he was regarding her with a devilish expression.

"May all your troubles be little ones," he began, and Jennifer clutched at his arm to stop him. She was off again, gasping, tears coming to her eyes, certain that any moment now they would be attracting attention. After all, what the hell could be so funny that it would reduce the two of them to hysterics in the middle of a banquet?

He opened his mouth, and she held up her hand. "Please," she whispered, "no more. I'm making a fool of myself as it is."

"And the road ahead paved with the fulfillment of your dreams," he recited rapidly.

Jennifer was helpless. She fell against him, and he grabbed her to steady her. After a moment she sobered, noticing the tenderness in his eyes.

"You really do like me, don't you?" he said softly. "You wish you didn't, but you do."

Jennifer's silence was her answer.

"I know the feeling," he said, releasing her. They stared at one another, an oasis of stillness in the bustling, crowded room.

Joe Thornridge arrived to break the spell. "Hi,

Jennifer," he said. "What's this guy been telling you?"

"Not much," Jennifer replied, realizing that that was possibly the biggest lie she had ever uttered.

"What's the matter with you, Chief? You boring this girl? I know a good one. Tell her about the time your knee gave out in the men's room at Grand Central Station."

"I think she could live without hearing that one, Joe," Lee said faintly.

"Aw, come on," Joe said, not to be dissuaded. "The Chief is, uh, using the facilities, if you know what I mean, when his leg folds up, and he goes crashing down between the sinks, flat out on the floor like a sack o' corn meal."

"Joe . . ." Lee said warningly.

"And so," Joe went on, warming to his tale, "Lee's all alone in there, can't get anybody to help him, and just has to wait for somebody to show."

Lee rolled his eyes, giving up.

"And guess who the first person to come in is?"

Jennifer was unable to guess.

"A cop!" Joe said, chortling. "In he walks and sees old superstar here grovelin' on the floor, mumbling about some trick knee. Thought it was some new form o' perversion, didn't he, Lee ol' boy?"

"If I killed him right now, how much time would they give me?" Lee said to Jennifer.

"Well, excuse me," Joe said, offended.

"It's all right, Joe," Lee said, clapping his friend on the back, "that just reminded me of something I've been meaning to tell the little Mrs. over there. About the time you and Carl Danbury got those two stewardesses and—"

Joe interrupted with an observation about some

people having no sense of humor and walked off, throwing Lee a black look over his shoulder.

Lee turned to Jennifer immediately. "Dance with me," he said.

This was a prospect too inviting to be denied. But just as Jennifer nodded, agreeing, the band switched from the slow numbers it had been playing to a heavy metal rendition of a popular rock tune, with a steady, underlying sensual rhythm.

Jennifer stopped short, intending to demur. But Lee's fingers closed around her wrist, and she looked up into his eyes. They contained an unmistakable challenge.

"Come on," he said softly. "You can't go back on it now."

Jennifer hesitated, but couldn't resist answering his unspoken dare. He wanted to dance? She would dance, all right.

Once they got out on the floor, all her inhibitions left her. Lee was as graceful dancing as he was playing football, and she matched him move for move, never breaking eye contact for a moment. As the music swelled, surrounding them, Jennifer felt it in her blood, carrying her away on a tide of reckless abandon. She leaned into Lee, shaking her shoulders, and saw the flicker of response in his eyes, as the crowd around them began to whistle and close in for a better look. He danced more provocatively, testing her, and she followed him, unwilling to back down. More people caught on to the show, and by the time the music ended, Lee and Jennifer had brought down the house, concluding to applause and wolf calls that left little doubt as to the nature of what had happened.

Jennifer walked straight off the floor, looking neither right nor left, until she reached her table and slid into her seat. Dolores was there, staring at her, dumbfounded.

"What's the matter, Dolores, you look like you need a drink," Jennifer said calmly.

"A drink!" Dolores yelped. "After that little scene, what I need is a cold shower. My God, Jen, what were you thinking of, to dance with him like that? I was ready to phone for the vice squad."

It wasn't easy to shock Dolores, but Jennifer had apparently done it. That was some sort of milestone. It also told Jennifer that if generally liberal Dolores reacted this way, the response in more conservative quarters (like the mind of Harold J. Salamone) might be somewhat greater.

Her chagrin was intensified by the return of Craig and John to their table. John glanced at Jennifer briefly and then looked down, fiddling with his napkin. Jennifer felt a sharp stab of sympathy for him. After all, she was his date, and she had just made a spectacle of herself with another man.

Jennifer felt the heat of a flush staining her skin and brushed damp tendrils of hair away from her face. "Excuse me," she mumbled, pushing back her chair. The men half rose out of their seats as she walked quickly through the ballroom until she reached the cool safety of the marble-floored entry hall.

The reception area was almost empty, as the party was in full swing. The clerk behind the desk glanced at her without curiosity, and one of the hostesses, who recognized her as being with the Freedom, merely nodded and walked on. Jennifer sank gratefully into a chair next to a large potted plant, and closed her eyes.

She had to get a grip on herself. This kind of behavior would never do. She was a mature, responsible, professional woman, not some love-struck adolescent tormented by spring fever. She knew how she felt about Lee, but the rest of the world didn't have to. If she kept on this way, the state of her affections would remain about as secret as tomorrow's headline on *The New York Times*.

She opened her eyes to see Lee standing in front of her, regarding her thoughtfully.

"Go away," she said and closed her eyes again.

"I intend to," he answered. "And you're coming with me."

Jennifer's eyes flew open.

"Let's ditch this place," he said, "and go for a ride."

"No."

"Why not? They're all getting loaded in there; nobody will miss us."

"I think Dawn and John might notice the empty seats if we leave, Lee." And draw their own conclusions after our recent performance, she added silently.

"Then we'll tell them a lie," he said simply.

She eyed him suspiciously.

"We'll say something has come up, that we have some work to do."

"Lee, anybody who swallows that will be ready to open a wooden nickel depository in the morning."

He grinned, sensing her weakening resistance. "Come on," he coaxed. "Live dangerously. We'll come back later. Play hooky, for a little while."

His terminology was appropriate. He sounded

exactly like one of her junior high buddies trying to convince her to skip school.

"You know you want to," he added softly.

Truer words were never spoken, Jennifer thought. He took her silence for assent, and she trailed after him, watching him stop at her table, and his own, to volunteer some story which undoubtedly no one believed.

She realized that he didn't care, and, with some surprise, that she really didn't, either. Her desire to be with Lee completely overrode the concern with appearances or propriety which might once have influenced her.

When he returned, she followed him wordlessly outside.

Lee took her back to his house, switching off a burglar alarm with a key as they entered. It was spotless, as always. He had mentioned that he had a cleaning service come in once a week, and Jennifer had noticed that he himself was very neat.

"I want to show you something upstairs," he said, leading the way. Jennifer went with him to the second floor, consisting of two large bedrooms, one of which was obviously Lee's, and another which looked as though it were used as a guest room. Jennifer glanced into the master bedroom as they passed. It was curiously plain, almost Spartan—an oversized bed and a color television on a stand the only touches of luxury. There was one whole wall of built-in closets, and another of floor to ceiling shelves filled with books.

At the end of the hall there was a short staircase, which led to the loft she'd glimpsed from below.

"The builders customized this for me," he commented as they ascended. "There are a number of artists in the complex, and they use the addition as a studio." He smiled over his shoulder at her. "I use it as a playroom."

Jennifer paused on the threshold of an immense circular room with a cathedral ceiling. Brightly colored, handwoven rugs were scattered on the polished oak floor, which gleamed with a rich luster. The room contained an impressive grand piano and three complicated-looking telescopes, their noses trained outward, poking through full-length, concealing drapes. There was also a plush couch set in a nook, with a companion coffee table covered with books and magazines. At the far end of the room stood a draftsman's table with an arc lamp anchored to shine on its inclined surface.

Jennifer walked over to the piano, running her hand over the beautiful cherry wood. "However did you get this up here?" she asked.

"There's a deck off the back, and the movers hoisted it to that level, and then pulled it in through the sliding glass doors."

Money could accomplish anything. She sifted through the stacks of sheet music which sat on a brass stand next to the instrument.

"I presume you play," she said.

Lee nodded. "One of the teachers at the Indian school taught me, and later I took lessons on my own." He pulled out the bench and sat on it, spreading his fingers over the keys. "She noticed the size of my hands when I was in her music class." He indicated an octave, and Jennifer could see that his fingers stretched two or three keys beyond that. "The reach makes it much easier to play." He winked. "Good for catching footballs, too." He

leaned back and flexed his arms elaborately, like
Victor Borge. "What would you like to hear?"

Jennifer had no idea. "Anything."

"Just what I like," Lee said. "A woman of univer-
sal tastes, easily pleased." He began with Beethoven's "Ode to Joy," playing with the ease of long
practice. He moved into a Chopin polonaise and
then to a series of Strauss waltzes.

Jennifer listened, enraptured.

Lee paused. "Enough of the highbrow stuff," he
said. "You like Gershwin?"

She smiled. "I love Gershwin."

He picked up the score from the movie *Manhat-
tan,* which was lying on top of the piano. "Gershwin
it is." Jennifer folded her arms on the cabinet and
leaned forward to study the musician as he played,
"S'Wonderful," "Rhapsody in Blue," "Embraceable
You," and "Someone to Watch Over Me" in a
medley, gliding from one to the other effortlessly. He
was absorbed, displaying the same concentration he
showed on the football field. Jennifer loved him so
much in that moment that she didn't trust herself to
speak.

He stopped, and she applauded, burlesquing her
reaction to cover her emotion.

He bowed from the waist. "I like the old tunes,"
he said. "Sometimes I play up here for hours. It's
very relaxing."

"It must be." He certainly covered the waterfront
in terms of variety. From Buddy Holly to Bruce
Springsteen to Beethoven and Gershwin was quite a
spread. "I'd like to hear more," she added.

He seemed pleased. "Sure." By heart, without
music, he played a haunting rendition of "Stardust,"
singing along in a clear, ringing baritone, and then

switched to "Deep Purple." He finished with the
theme from *Casablanca*, and Jennifer watched as the
last notes of "As Time Goes By" faded into silence.
Lee sat looking at his hands, clenched in his lap.

"If I had closed my eyes, I would have thought
you were Dooley Wilson," Jennifer said lightly.

Lee looked up abruptly, as if roused from some
reverie. "Oh, yes, thank you." He was silent a
moment longer, and then said, "I shouldn't play that,
it always gets me down."

"Why?"

"Oh, you know, the movie, Bogart and Bergman,
so in love, but so wrong for each other, caught in
such an impossible situation. Sad, don't you think?"

Jennifer turned away, not wanting him to see the
impact of his remark on her face. "Yes, very sad,"
she commented neutrally.

He got up and moved to a switch on the wall.
"And now for the *pièce de resistance*," he said. He
touched the button, and all the drapes pulled back
from the windows at once, revealing floor to ceiling
glass completely around the room. The loft was
actually on the roof of the townhouse, so the night
sky surrounded them in all directions. Jennifer felt
bathed in stars.

He waited for her reaction. When none came, he
said, "Well?"

"I'm speechless."

"An historic occasion," he said dryly.

Jennifer spun around in a circle, observing the
heavens from every direction. "I never knew there
were so many stars."

"You can see them better here because you're
high up and there's no light competing with them,

like from malls and parking lots." He paused. "In Montana, on the Northern plains where I lived, on a summer night the stars would press in on you, so close, and so many . . ." He stopped. "Did you ever see one of those glass paperweights kids have, when you turn it upside down, it looks like a snowfall?"

"Yes."

"Well, the only way I can describe the experience is that you feel like you're in one of those domes, with the stars surrounding you instead of the snow."

Jennifer felt her throat constrict with sympathy at his tone. She had never realized before that he was very homesick.

"I'm sure it's beautiful," she said.

He went to the biggest telescope and crooked his finger at her, squinting into the eyepiece. "Come here and look at this," he said.

Jennifer did as she was bid, bending to gaze through the lens. Lee stood directly behind her, talking into her ear, his hands on her shoulders. She was acutely conscious of the warmth of his fingers on her bare skin above the neckline of the dress, the closeness of his lips as he spoke.

"Do you see that over there?" he asked. "That's not a star, it's the planet Venus. Notice how it doesn't twinkle, but seems to shine with a steady light. That's how you can tell the difference. And look at the Big Dipper," he added, swinging the scope to a different angle, pointing out various stars and constellations. She recognized some of the names from long-ago, half-forgotten science classes: Arcturus and Betelgeuse, Cassiopeia and Sirius and Orion. He knew them all, and their locations, how they shifted position in the sky through the year. The scope was on rollers, and he moved it about with them as he spoke, to give her a better view of what he was describing. Jennifer caught his enthusiasm and studied everything carefully, intrigued.

"Now this one," he said, leading her to another scope, "is more powerful, a high-intensity scope. If you look directly at the sun through one of these, you'll go blind. I have a special filter to use, but even then you have to be careful because sometimes the filters burn through, and . . ." he trailed off, leaving the sentence unfinished. Then he said, "I'm sorry. I'm showing off and I'm boring you."

Jennifer looked up at him, saw the concerned face, the intent, expressive eyes, and said, "You could never bore me." It was out before she could stop it.

She saw him draw a breath and lean toward her. Aware that she had made a mistake, she walked away, out of reach. "What's in there?" she asked, pointing to a cedar chest behind the piano, changing the subject.

For a minute he didn't answer, and she feared that he wouldn't allow her to evade him. But then his voice came, low, intimate. "I'll show you."

He lifted the lid, and brought out a leather shirt, encrusted with elaborate beadwork, and several other items of clothing, obviously old and hand-made.

"These belonged to my great-grandfather," he said. "I wish I could wear them, but they're too small for me."

Jennifer touched the numerous, brightly colored decorations. "What are these?"

"Porcupine quills. The animals weren't too plentiful on the plains, so the quills were highly prized. The Blackfeet used to get them in trade from other tribes."

"It's a shame they don't fit you."

"Yeah, well, I'm considerably bigger than my ancestors," he said, laying the garments carefully back in the chest. "It must be those French genes." He stood and tapped his very straight, very European nose. "I think they're responsible for this, too."

"You're part French?"

"My grandmother married a French Canadian trapper, Jacques Beaufort. My parents have a tintype of him back home, a great big guy with a formidable moustache. They say he had a team of sled dogs that could make it through the worst weather British Columbia had to offer, and let me tell you, that's pretty bad." He dropped the lid on the chest and came back to her, taking both her hands in his. "I guess I've shown you all my treasures, haven't I?"

"I guess so. You have some solitary hobbies, for a man who could buy anything he wants."

He tightened his grip on her hands. "I do wind up spending a lot of time alone, but I prefer it that way. Most of the people who like me now, like me for the wrong reasons. I feel most comfortable with the friends who knew me before all this happened, this football jive." He smiled slightly. "The people who loved you when you had nothing are the people who really care."

Like Dawn, Jennifer thought miserably. It wasn't fair. If Jennifer had known him before, she would have loved him just as much. Was it her fault that it was his sports career that brought them together?

Jennifer disengaged herself, stepping back. "Dawn Blacktree told me you were once in love with her sister."

Lee moved forward, keeping the same distance between them. "Oh, we were all kids together, back home," he said evasively. "Dawn's family was very good to me at a time in my life when I really needed help."

"She's very pretty," Jennifer said.

"Yes, she is," Lee answered, watching Jennifer carefully.

"Is that what her name means in Pikuni, Dawn?"

"The literal translation is 'Appearing Day.'"

"Appearing Day. How lovely."

Lee put his hand on her shoulder. "Jen . . ."

She tried to walk past him. "No. Go get one of the old-timers who really care. I'm one of the late arrivals, remember, the ones who only like you for your image and your money," she said bitterly.

Lee caught her and pulled her against his chest. "I didn't mean that to include you, paleface," he whispered. "I never saw anyone as spectacularly unimpressed as you were with the whole scene. I know you're not like that."

Jennifer relaxed against him, letting her head fall to his shoulder. His arms enclosed her, strong and warm.

"Kiss me, Jen," he said huskily. "Just once, and then we'll leave. I promise."

He didn't have to say it again. She was lifting her lips to his as he bent his head.

He broke his promise, kissing her again and again until she was weak and clinging to him for support. He half carried her to the couch, dropping onto it with her, drawing her under him. His mouth moved everywhere he could reach, his hands searching for the zipper at the back of her dress, his body hard and urgent against hers. She knew that if she didn't stop him soon, she wouldn't stop him at all.

"Lee," she gasped, tearing her mouth from his, "We can't. We have to get back."

He held her fast, still caressing her. "Do we?" he said, agonized. "Do we?"

"Yes," she insisted, pulling away from him, trying to modulate her voice and regain control. "Think of Dawn, think of John waiting there for us. It's bad enough that we took off the way we did, but if we don't return it will be so much worse. I know I hurt John already tonight, I don't want to add to it."

He didn't answer, but he stood and smoothed his hair with trembling fingers. Then he offered her his hand and pulled her to her feet, releasing her the instant she got her balance.

"Let's go," he said shortly, and she followed him out of the room. She passed the draftsman's table and noticed that he had a map of the heavens pinned to it, with the trajectory patterns of various stars traced on it with a compass. She thought of him sitting there, patiently plotting the courses of celestial bodies and almost burst into tears. She was in a bad way. Even his hobbies were touching, infinitely precious and incredibly dear.

Jennifer walked down the steps behind Lee like a woman who was in a lot of trouble, and knew it.

The party was breaking up when they got back to the hotel. It had been a silent ride from Lee's house, and Jennifer walked in ahead of Lee, looking for Dolores. She didn't glance back to see where he went.

Dolores and Craig and John were in the lobby. John didn't ask her anything, just said that he was going out to get his car. Craig went with him.

Dolores pinned her to the wall as soon as the men were out of earshot. "Where the hell did you go?" she hissed. "It was not lost on the group at large that the two of you vanished at the same time."

"What do you mean? Didn't Lee say where we were going?" Jennifer hedged.

Dolores made a disgusted noise. "I wouldn't even repeat the threadbare fairy tale he told us before you left. Jennifer, what's going on?"

"Nothing is going on," Jennifer said wearily. "He just took me to his house to see some telescopes."

Dolores looked at her as if she were demented. "Telescopes?"

"Yes, yes, it's his hobby; he's an amateur astronomer. He wanted to show me the stars."

"Show you the stars? Well, that's original, at least, a new variation on an old theme. It used to be 'come up and see my etchings,' now it's 'come up and see my asteroids.'"

Jennifer fixed her with a deadly look. "Dolores, for my sake, could you try, just once, not to be such a smartass?"

Dolores stared at her, releasing her breath slowly in an inaudible sigh. "Oh, Jen, you poor thing. You've fallen for him, haven't you?"

Jennifer said nothing.

"Please, be careful."

"I'm trying."

Dolores dropped her eyes. "Well, I guess that's all you can do."

The men came back, and Jennifer went with John.

He was silent as they drove through the downtown streets toward Yardley, and Jennifer began to feel that if he didn't say something soon, she was going to scream.

"Did you have a good time?" she asked brightly.

"Fine."

"I hope Dolores kept you entertained while I was gone."

"Dolores could keep anybody entertained, even a dull, unglamorous legal type like me."

"John, I . . ."

He took one hand off the steering wheel to hold it up for silence. "Don't say it, Jennifer. Don't demean yourself, and me. You think I can't see what he has, that I don't? I know what's going on, give me that much credit at least. If you had ever once looked at me the way you were looking at him tonight, we would have been married long ago. Just drop it, okay?"

Jennifer dropped it.

The night had turned cool, in the manner of late summer, and Jennifer built a fire when she got home. She was too keyed up to sleep and didn't even undress, but made herself a cup of tea and curled up on the living room sofa to think.

The trouble was, she couldn't think. All her legal training in logic and the systematic breakdown of a problem had deserted her and left her mind as blank as an unused sheet of paper. What good was an education if you couldn't use it to help yourself? She had used it to help others, but in her case, emotion took over and made a mockery of the rationality she had worked so hard to obtain.

She lifted her head when she heard the sound of a motor in her driveway. Mrs. Mason went to bed at ten o'clock and never had night visitors. Who could it be, at this hour?

And then she knew. A hollow grew at the pit of her stomach, and she set her cup down carefully, so as not to spill it. She made herself walk slowly to the door and was ready when the knock came.

Lee stood on the tiny porch, still dressed in the evening clothes he had worn earlier.

"I'm back," he said.

"I see."

"I wasn't sure if you'd still be up."

"I am."

They stared at one another, illuminated by the yellow glow of the porch light.

"I . . . may I come in? I need to talk to somebody." He stopped, and then raised his eyes to hers. "No, that isn't true. I need to talk to *you.*"

She stepped aside, and as he walked past her she said, "Are you hungry? I can fix something."

They were whispering, like two conspirators. "Thanks. I'm afraid I didn't eat much tonight."

That makes two of us, Jennifer thought. As she reached to shut the door behind them, she caught sight of one of the stars Lee had shown her, twinkling by itself against a velvet background of night sky.

" 'First star on the right, and straight on 'til morning,' " she said softly.

Lee turned to look back at her. "What?"

Jennifer pointed to the star. "It's from *Peter Pan,* the directions to Never Never Land."

He smiled down at her. "Is that where you want to go?"

Jennifer gazed up at him, as magical, to her at least, as any boy in a children's tale who was ageless and could fly.

"I think I'm already there."

6

It was hours before Jennifer realized that they still hadn't eaten, but Lee seemed unaware of it. He was more talkative than she had ever seen him, discussing his background more freely than he usually did. He was troubled by his choice to play professional football, which had been made ten years before but apparently still weighed heavily on his mind.

"If I had gone to medical school," he said thoughtfully, "I'd be just starting now. In this business, I'm on my way out. You can't stand being beaten up every Sunday for an unlimited amount of time. I think I'm approaching the limit."

"Why *didn't* you go to medical school?" Jennifer asked.

"Because I love to play football," he answered simply. "And I thought if I could be paid, and paid well, to do what I love to do, then that would be the best life anyone could want."

Jennifer smiled. "Oh, yes."

He sighed. "But that was a decision I made a long while ago, when all I could see was money and a good time. Now I wonder if I did the right thing. Any career in sports is a short one. What will I do in a few more seasons when all this is over? My life has been devoted to, as you correctly pointed out to me once, a children's game. If I'd been a doctor, I could have done some good, gone back to Montana, worked on the reservation, in the schools. I could have done some good," he repeated. He shook his head. "It's funny how, the older you get, the less the material things matter, the more important a sense of accomplishment becomes."

Jennifer studied him, touched to the heart.

"You should feel a sense of accomplishment," she said. "You've risen to the top in a difficult field, in which the competition is fierce. And I don't agree that you could have done more for your people as a doctor. Then you might have healed them, true, but now you are a symbol of success to American Indians everywhere. Think of the little boys all over the country looking up to you for what they might become. I'm sure you're an inspiration to them all."

He swallowed hard, looking down. "I . . . thank you. I needed to hear that today," he said huskily.

She reached for his hand, and he gripped her fingers convulsively.

"That dream has never left you, has it?" she said.

He shrugged. "I guess it never has."

"Then do something about it."

He looked up at her, astonished. "Like what? I'm thirty two years old, for Christ's sake."

"A great age, to be sure," Jennifer responded dryly. "I'm certain that some school would take you. You're famous, Lee. Think of the boost to the reputation of the school. And you told me your grades were good."

He waved his hand, dismissing the notion. "That was another life. I could never live like a student again. I would have to take entrance exams, compete against kids fresh out of college."

"I didn't say it would be easy," Jennifer said. "Of course, if you're afraid to try . . ."

That comment produced the desired result. "That's not the issue!" Lee said fiercely. "And I wouldn't want any special privileges, either."

She blinked at him.

"*If* I were going to attempt it, *which* I'm not," he said pointedly. "And I don't want to discuss it any further."

"Certainly, your majesty."

"Don't get sarcastic, Jenny. It doesn't become you." He changed the subject. "I have to go to New York on Thursday."

"That's nice."

"Not very. The place depresses me. It lacks the ambiance one sees in the perfume commercials. It always seems to be filled with heroin addicts with permanent head colds, and coke freaks with permanent nosebleeds."

"Oh, come on. It isn't that bad."

"No? You ever walked through the Bowery on a Saturday night in summer?"

"I can't say that I have."

"Looks like the last act of Hamlet. Bodies everywhere."

Jennifer laughed. "I'd have guessed that your experiences there were limited to lunches at Elaine's and nights with the in-crowd at the best clubs."

"You'd be wrong," he said shortly, in a voice which did not encourage her to ask questions.

He glanced at his watch. "It's late, or very early. I should go."

Jennifer said nothing. She didn't want him to leave, but how could she risk another scene?

He got up and reached for his jacket. She followed him to the door.

"Thanks for listening," he said.

"Thanks for talking," she whispered.

Lee stood looking down at her. He reached out to smooth her hair back from her face. His fingers trailed across her brow to her cheek. Unable to stop herself, Jennifer turned her head and kissed his palm.

He froze.

"Don't go," she murmured. "Don't go."

"I'm not going anywhere," he said firmly. He dropped his jacket on a chair and picked her up as if she were weightless, walking to the sofa in front of the fire. He sat upon it with her still in his arms.

Jennifer clung to him, her arms about his neck. His eyes, heavy lidded, thickly lashed, gazed down at her, lambent. They closed slowly as his mouth met hers.

His kiss was forceful, demanding, right from the start. He was sure, this time, that she would not stop him.

She could not have done so if she'd tried. Jennifer was so in love with him that one night together was preferable to a lifetime of wondering what might have been. She knew the chance she was taking, but it no longer mattered. The only thing in the world was this man, and this moment.

The feel of his hands on her body was the strongest erotic stimulant she had ever known. Jennifer could not get enough of him; her own aggression surprised her and aroused Lee. She tore her lips from his and pressed them to his throat, slipping her hands inside his clothes. He groaned and shifted her weight on his lap, pulling her closer.

Jennifer unbuttoned his shirt with trembling fingers, and he shrugged it off, letting it fall to the floor.

His skin was smooth, perfect, golden bronze. He half lay against the cushions, head thrown back, eyes closed, as she kissed and caressed him, stroking the hard, muscular arms and shoulders, rasping his flat dark nipples with her tongue.

It was not enough. Her hands strayed below his waist, and his breath hissed through his teeth. He moved to get up, to undress. Besotted, she hung on him, unable to bear the loss of contact.

He gently put her hands away, and quickly shed the rest of his clothes. Jennifer sat, drugged, until he returned in seconds, to disrobe her like a doll. As he removed each garment, he mouthed the part of her body he had uncovered. She put her fist in her mouth to prevent crying out, and he pulled it back, kissing the curled fingers. "I want to hear," he whispered.

When she was naked, he scooped her up in his arms again and carried her to the hearth rug before the fire. He dropped beside her.

"Please," she whimpered. "Please."

"Anything," he murmured, running his palm over her full breasts, her flat belly, absorbing the beauty of her body.

"Love me. Now."

He crushed her to him. "I will," he groaned. "I do."

He stroked her thighs, and they opened to receive him. She gazed in mute adoration at his face above hers, his lower lip caught between his teeth in a spasm of pleasure as he entered her. They both gasped aloud with the sensation.

Jennifer clutched him, burying her face against his shoulder as he moved within her. Tears stung behind her lids and ached unshed in her throat. She must not cry. She wanted to remember everything. Everything.

She was certain that she would.

The cold woke Jennifer a few hours later. The fire had died, and the room become chilly. A few fading embers still glowed on the hearth, but they gave little heat.

Lee slept face down, one arm thrown across her, a long muscular leg entwined with hers. She slipped away from him, and he stirred with the movement. Jennifer went to the hall closet to get a robe, and when she returned, he was sitting up, looking at her.

She felt a deep flush creep up her neck. What did he think of her? What did she think of herself? She had never been so brazen. He probably thought . . . she didn't want to think what he probably thought.

To cover her embarrassment and confusion, she grabbed a poker and stirred the fire.

"Let me do that," he said, adding logs from the storage bin in the wall. Soon the blaze was roaring again.

He reclined once more on the rug, looking like an Inca prince with his sleek, strong limbs, carved features, and midnight hair. He reached up for her with one hand and drew her down to him.

"What's this?" he asked, fingering her housecoat.

"I was cold."

"Take if off," he said huskily. "I'll make you warm."

She obeyed and closed her eyes, letting herself melt into him. "We should move to the bedroom," she said. "You won't get any rest."

"I'm not interested in rest," he said huskily. "I'm fine right here."

He propped himself on one elbow and gazed down at her, tracing her features with a blunt forefinger. Then he bent to place a kiss on the tip of her nose before he moved his mouth lower, seeking her lips with his.

The cycle began again, as headlong and as powerful as before. All her concerns went out of her mind. She would worry about them later.

It was dawn before they slept—the deep, exhausted sleep of satiety.

7

~~~~~~~~~~~~~~~~~~~~~~~~~~~~

Jennifer woke first in the morning and showered while Lee was still asleep. She dressed in jeans and a blouse and walked past Lee's prone form on the way through the hall to the kitchen. He lay sprawled on the hearth rug, the arm which had claimed her so possessively during the night still flung out at his side. The sight of him filled her with yearning tenderness, and she could have stood there, watching him, all day. But she deliberately moved on, making coffee as quietly as possible.

A kiss on the back of her neck told her that Lee was standing behind her. As usual, she had not heard his approach. She set down the box of filters she was holding and turned to face him.

He was bare chested and barefoot, clad only in the black formal pants he had worn to the reception. His hair was still mussed and his eyes heavy from the night, making him look boyish and vulnerable, but never more attractive. Jennifer had to fight to keep from embracing him.

He embraced her instead, drawing her against his chest. The feel of his silky skin, the enclosing warmth of his muscular arms, sent her spinning into the now familiar vortex of desire. She resisted it, evading his attempt to kiss her.

Feeling her reluctance, Lee held her away from

him, searching her face. His unasked question hung between them, demanding an answer.

Jennifer dropped her eyes from his. "I'm afraid, Lee. This is all too much, ever since we met, the constant pull, and now last night . . ." She broke off, unable to articulate further, finally repeating, "I'm afraid."

She half expected him to ask what there was to fear, or otherwise dismiss her concern. But he surprised her, releasing her and looking away. She saw him draw a slow, careful breath.

"And you think I'm not?" he said quietly.

His reply produced a mixed reaction in Jennifer. She felt a surge of joy at the knowledge that he was apparently taking their relationship as seriously as she was. She would have been devastated by any light treatment on his part of what was so important to her. But at the same time, she felt something like despair. He couldn't guide her out of these troubled waters; he was drowning, too.

Jennifer studied his strong profile, as sharp and as clean as any etched on a coin, and said softly, "I don't do this, Lee, and I'm getting in too deep. I can't help it. I'm not much for one-night stands."

He raised his eyes to her face. "I know that," he said seriously. "Don't you think I know that?"

Jennifer nodded, relieved. "But where does that leave us?" she asked. "What's the sense in torturing ourselves with samples of what we can't have on a permanent basis? You've already told me how you feel about your sister, and I can't be a party to the sort of betrayal you think she has made of her background and her people. I know you don't want that, and if you got involved with me you'd wind up hating yourself in the end."

He said nothing.

Jennifer had almost hoped that he would protest, but she saw now that he wasn't going to. She could never affect his deepest beliefs; they were strongly held, rooted in his soul. There was an inner core of mysticism in him, which she had glimpsed while he talked to the children that afternoon, born of an ancient way of life as foreign to her as the pyramids of Egypt. That will, and that difference, could never be possessed. She loved him and respected him for it, but knew that no matter how much he wanted her, he couldn't change.

"We're just wrong for each other, and it's nobody's fault. Your heritage is very important to you, and you need someone who understands it and can share it. You'll always be afraid I'll turn you into one of those imitation WASPs you despise, make you forget who you are. And I've been burned once, I'm gun-shy, too. Let's call it quits now, before we hurt each other." Jennifer said all this calmly, without betraying the inner turmoil she felt, which increased with each word.

He still didn't answer.

"Say something, Lee."

He lifted one shoulder. "What can I say? You've said it all."

So that was to be it, then. Lee left the room and returned wearing his ruffled shirt, unbuttoned to the waist, and carrying his jacket draped over his shoulder, hooked by one index finger. He cupped her chin in his free hand, looking at her as if he might never see her again.

"That is such a sweet face," he said, and kissed her gently on the mouth.

"Thank you for last night," he said. "I won't forget it."

He was terribly close to saying final things, and Jennifer held her breath. But he merely brushed his lips across her brow, and slipped quietly out the door.

Jennifer stood with her eyes closed, still feeling his touch on her skin. She'd handled it well, behaved reasonably and with great maturity. But that knowledge did not ease the pain she had masked so expertly for Lee's benefit.

She still wanted him desperately and didn't know what to do about it.

Jennifer spent the morning in a state of suspended animation, going through the motions of doing laundry and dusting furniture like an automaton. When the phone rang around lunchtime, her heart stopped for a second, but then she knew it wouldn't be Lee.

It was Marilyn. They exchanged news and small talk for a little while, and then Marilyn said, in that gently probing way she had, "Something's wrong, Jen. What is it?"

Jennifer bluffed around for a while, but didn't fool Marilyn for a minute. She finally blurted out that Lee had spent the night with her.

There was a long pause at the other end of the line. Then Marilyn said in crisp, businesslike tones, "I'll be right over."

Jennifer heard the click of disconnection before she could protest.

Marilyn arrived to find Jennifer in the middle of cleaning out her drawers, and items of clothing and other miscellany were strewn about the bedroom in untidy piles. She surveyed the chaos and shook her head.

"Trying to work off our frustrations, are we?"

"Failing," Jennifer responded, tossing a mateless sock into a laundry basket with others of its kind. She looked up. "Where's Jeff?"

"With a sitter," Marilyn answered. "I thought we should conduct this conversation without interruption." She looked around. "Come out to the living room. You're doing more harm than good in here anyway."

Jennifer got up off her knees and followed Marilyn into the other room. Marilyn plopped into a chair and put her feet up on the coffee table.

"Okay, sweetie. Give."

Jennifer recounted everything that had happened since the morning of the previous day, including the conversation she and Lee had had before he left. Marilyn listened, interrupting only with an occasional pertinent question or brief comment. When Jennifer was all talked out, Marilyn leaned forward and peered at her owlishly.

"Is that it?"

Jennifer nodded.

"So. As I understand it, the problem is that he feels a relationship with you would go against his whole background and way of life. Has he said this?"

Jennifer made a frustrated gesture. "He doesn't have to say it, I know him, I know what he thinks. He would really like to go back and work on the reservation in Montana, and I'd be totally out of place there. In some small, atavistic part of his mind, the part that remembers things it has never seen, I will always be esumissa, a white woman, the enemy."

"Jennifer, that's absurd," Marilyn said gently.

"Is it? The Blackfeet hated whites, wouldn't trade with them, never took white captives. I've been reading about them."

"You're talking about the attitudes of one hundred and fifty years ago!" Marilyn said.

"So what? If you were in his position, would you forget? What was done, and who did it?"

"*You* didn't do it!" Marilyn almost shouted. "When the Indians were being exterminated your ancestors were up to their necks in some peat bog, as poor and as persecuted as his!"

Jennifer shook her head. "That doesn't matter. He looks at me, and sees somebody who'll want him to turn his back on what he is. You should have seen his face when he was talking about his sister, about the imitation WASPs. The contempt, the bitterness in his voice. He talked about the marriages he's seen between Indians and non-Indians in which the Indian always gives up his past and adopts his spouse's culture."

"He may not have been saying that for your benefit."

"I was the only one there, Marilyn," Jennifer said dryly.

"Well, did you tell him you'd never ask him to do that?"

Marilyn's obtuseness was getting on Jennifer's nerves. "Of course I'd never *ask* him to do that. I wouldn't have to. It's a subtle process of erosion of spirit, and only one of his own people could prevent that from happening." She snorted. "And just by the merest chance, one of them has shown up, on cue, to drive the big bad bogeywoman away." Jennifer told Marilyn about Dawn, and her past relationship with Lee.

"But you're not sure anything is going on between them."

"No, I'm not. But I noticed something at his house that only half registered at the time, and the more I think about it, the surer I am that Dawn is staying with Lee."

"What do you mean?"

"Well, when I was there I passed this sort of guest room that he has, and there were bags on the floor, and personal items about, as if someone were occupying it. And I think I know who that someone is."

Marilyn waved her hand in the air. "That doesn't prove anything. You said she was an old friend. If he has the room, why shouldn't she stay there?"

"I know, I know. But the idea of it doesn't make me too happy."

Marilyn pulled at her lower lip thoughtfully. "Has it occurred to you that he might be using this Dawn as a shield, retreating to the familiar in defense against his feelings for you?"

Jennifer rubbed her forehead distractedly. "Even if that's true, how does it help me? I don't want to be someone he has to erect barriers against for fear of losing his identity. And I'll tell you something else. Even if I could transform myself into a full-blooded Siksikai, I wouldn't do it. I have my pride, too. If he can't take me as I am, and accept me for what I am, then he has no real regard for me anyway."

Marilyn smiled. "Spoken like Seamus Gardiner's daughter."

"Up the rebels," Jennifer responded, and they both laughed.

Marilyn glanced at the clock on the wall. "I've got to go, I was only able to get Barbara to stay with Jeff for a couple of hours." She regarded Jennifer closely. "Are you going to be all right?"

"Of course. I'll deal with it."

Marilyn didn't look convinced. "Call me if you feel like you want to talk again."

"I will."

The apartment seemed very empty after Marilyn left. Jennifer trudged back to the bedroom to dig out from under the avalanche, hoping that the work would make her tired enough to sleep.

The season began, and Lee's personal appearances came to an end as the games got underway. Jennifer didn't see him anymore in connection with work and after the manner of their last parting, she knew he wouldn't call her. So she contented herself with memories of their night together and spent a lot of time daydreaming, lost in thought.

"You look tired," Dolores said bluntly one morning. They were settling down to work in Jennifer's office.

Jennifer *was* tired. She found herself taking naps at odd times, but ascribed the fatigue to depression.

When Jennifer didn't respond, Dolores tried another tack. "I saw your ex on a talk show last night," she said brightly. "He's taking flying lessons."

"From what I remember of his drinking habits, he will rarely need a plane," Jennifer answered.

"Hostility," Dolores said. "A lot of hostility there, Jen." Dolores had been attending an encounter group and was lately given to such observations.

"My experience with Bob entitles me to a little

hostility," Jennifer said. "Now are we going to get these letters out, or what?"

Dolores ignored the question and started snapping dead leaves off the Swedish ivy plant hanging in the window. "Have you seen Lee Youngson since the company dinner?" she asked, too casually.

"No."

Dolores tossed the brown vegetation into the trash, wiping her hands on her skirt. "So that is the reason for this funk."

"Dolores—" Jennifer began.

Dolores stabbed an index finger at her. "No, Jen, don't shut me up. I may not be Einstein, but anyone can see that something is wrong with you. You're going around like an extra on the set of *The Night of the Living Dead*. Don't you plan on doing anything about it?"

Jennifer turned in her swivel chair and deliberately looked out the window. "No."

Dolores folded her arms and leaned against Jennifer's desk. "It's not one-sided, you know."

Jennifer revolved back in her direction.

Dolores fluffed her hair with her fingers. "Did you ever see that old movie with Bing Crosby and Grace Kelly?"

Oh, God. Was this going to be another one of Dolores' flights of fancy? Jennifer was in no mood for "Hollywood Squares" today.

"Which one?" Jennifer said patiently.

"Ah, let me see, I can't think . . . oh, yes. *The Country Girl.* It's about an alcoholic actor and his wife, and the director who falls in love with her."

"Sure, I remember it. Grace Kelly won an Oscar."

"Well, the husband knows his wife and the direc-

tor are in love, but they're trying to hide it. And at
one point he says to them, 'The only thing more
obvious than two people looking longingly at one
another is two people trying not to.'" Dolores
looked meaningfully at Jennifer. "I was watching the
two of you at the Stratford, and for some reason,
that line just came to mind."

Jennifer got the message. Every once in a while
Dolores surprised her. It was easy to forget that
behind that airhead exterior was a keen observer of
the human condition.

"Why aren't you going after him?" Dolores persisted.

Jennifer sighed. "It's . . . complicated, Dolores."

Dolores looked skeptical. "It must be. But I'll tell
you one thing, if he were as interested in me as he
seems to be in you, *I* wouldn't be spending my days
in a trance."

That was undoubtedly true. Dolores was never
one to let any grass grow under her feet where men
were concerned.

"I believe you. Now can we get to these letters?"

Dolores whipped out her steno pad and waved it
under Jennifer's nose, muttering under her breath,
and then sat with her pen poised above the paper,
waiting.

Jennifer set to work.

Jennifer persuaded Marilyn to go to a Freedom
game with her the following weekend. At first
Marilyn hesitated, thinking that it would be rubbing
salt in Jennifer's wounds to see Lee play. But
Jennifer's insistence became pathetic. It was obvious
that Jennifer needed to see Lee, even if it was from a
distance, and Marilyn eventually gave in to her.

Jennifer used her connections to get seats on the fifty yard line, reserved for a season ticket holder who would be out of town for the weekend. They were right behind the Freedom's bench and had a clear view of the players.

Marilyn's knowledge of football was even more limited than Jennifer's, which meant that it was meager indeed. She spent the entire game jabbing Jennifer in the ribs, asking "What's going on?" and "Why are they doing that?" Jennifer usually didn't know the answer, and so a lot of what happened down below sailed right over their heads. But they made up in enthusiastic response what they lacked in understanding.

Lee was called out of the game for a rest during the second quarter. He took off his helmet and sat hunched forward with his elbows on his knees, staring at the game. Jennifer could see that his hair was plastered to his skull with perspiration. An assistant coach came by and handed him a towel, and Lee rubbed his head briskly with it, then left it draped around his neck. He went back to watching the action on the field, nodding as another player bent to say something to him in passing.

The Freedom was ahead 21–7 at the break. Jennifer and Marilyn went to get soft drinks during the half time show.

"Has it helped to see him?" Marilyn asked as they sipped soda and watched the crowd milling around them.

"I don't know," Jennifer answered. "I do know that I feel like a voyeur, watching him this way."

Marilyn made a face. "If you're a voyeur, so are the fifty thousand other people in the stands with us."

Jennifer crumpled her waxy cup and tossed it in a receptacle. "You know what I mean."

Marilyn acknowledged that she did.

The game had resumed by the time they got back to their seats. They arrived just in time to see Lee make a spectacular run as the crowd leaped, screaming, to its feet. Marilyn was riveted, motionless, as she watched Lee outwit and outmaneuver his way downfield.

"He's poetry in motion, isn't he?" she said to Jennifer, raising her voice to make herself heard over the surrounding noise.

"Yes, he is."

She continued to watch as Lee was finally brought to the ground. It took three opposing players to do it.

"I've never seen anything like it," Marilyn commented as the teams reassembled and the onlookers took their seats again, quieting down for the next play.

Jennifer had to laugh. "Of course, you haven't. You've never seen a football game."

But Marilyn wasn't listening, as caught up as the rest of the fans in anticipation of another dazzling display.

Jennifer smiled to herself. Another convert.

The Freedom won, 28–14.

The two women went to Bookbinder's for dinner. They were lucky to get in without a reservation, but they ate early, right after the game, before the evening rush.

Marilyn had baked scrod and Jennifer had oyster stew. Marilyn watched Jennifer crumbing crackers into her untouched soup and said, "Why don't you call him?"

Jennifer closed her eyes. That suggestion ranked right up there with the offer of a cruise on the Titanic.

"All right, all right, don't call him. Let's take a walk to the Newmarket instead, look around at the shops. That'll take your mind off him."

Jennifer doubted it, but as an idea it was an improvement over the first one. Marilyn ate as Jennifer toyed with her food awhile longer, and then they walked out into the early autumn dusk.

Society Hill was busy on this Saturday night, with couples strolling hand in hand, and families out for a little exercise. A brisk breeze blew in from the nearby Delaware, making it seem cooler than it actually was. Jennifer and Marilyn cruised the stores, and Jennifer charged a lace shawl she couldn't afford in an effort to lift her spirits. They would plunge again when she got the bill.

They left the shopping area and walked through the restored section fronting the river, which was paved with brick and sported colonial streetlamps and reproduced period facades on the houses. One block from the water was a new condominium complex, a high-rise, where the apartments cost a fortune. Harold Salamone lived there, along with several of the city's top businessmen.

"How about going to Scruples with me tonight?" Marilyn said brightly as they crossed the street to stand looking out across the bay. "Jeff's staying with my mother and I have the evening free."

"Marilyn, it is not necessary to supervise me."

"Who's supervising?" Marilyn said innocently. "You know that guy I met, Jim, the Ph.D. student at Villanova?"

"Mmm-hmm. Clinical psychology, wasn't it?"

"That's right. He works nights as a bartender at Scruples."

Jennifer chuckled. "Ah-hah. And here I thought you were unselfishly devoting every thought to my welfare."

"I am, I am. Trying to kill two birds with one stone, that's all."

"I see. Well, I hate to disappoint you, but I'm bushed. I'm going to take a relaxing bath and go to bed early."

Marilyn turned and faced her, outraged. "You mean you'd make me go alone? You won't even come along to offer moral support? Some friend."

"Marilyn, that's emotional blackmail."

Marilyn grinned triumphantly. "Let's go home and change."

Jennifer's enthusiasm for the project began to pick up while she was getting ready to go. She had a new dress she'd never worn, a soft silk sheath in a frosty ice blue. She put it on and donned her new shawl.

Marilyn came for Jennifer in her vintage Pinto, and they were on their way back to Philly. This is how I spend my life, Jennifer thought, shuttling back and forth to the City of Brotherly Love.

Scruples was in the middle of the block at Second and South. As they passed under the awning at the entrance, it began to rain. It had been raining on and off for days, stopping just long enough to allow the Freedom to play the game that afternoon, and it looked as though it would be a wet night.

Scruples was jammed. The music blared and the strobe lights flashed, assaulting Jennifer's ears and eyes and almost prompting an about-face for the door. Marilyn seized her arm and propelled her along to the bar, where her friend was serving drinks. They waited in a crowd three deep to get to him.

Jennifer looked around, trying to spot an empty table. She brushed off several approaches, including one by a character who told her that he was a government agent involved in "very important work." Jennifer sent him back to Washington.

Marilyn went off on her own, pushing through the mass of humanity. Jennifer craned her neck and saw that Marilyn had reached her quarry by wedging between two people who appeared to be having an argument. Jim looked up and greeted Marilyn with a welcoming smile. Jennifer silently wished them a wedding in June and shoved her way to a table just vacated by a couple who vanished into the crush.

She was no sooner seated than she was joined by a man so drunk she couldn't believe he was standing on his feet. He was tipping his drink, obviously the latest in a long line, to one side, and with every movement it sloshed onto his hand. He didn't seem to notice.

Jennifer had difficulty understanding what he was saying, not that she wanted to in any case. The music and his intoxication combined to make him almost incomprehensible. She picked up that his name was George, and his intentions became clear when he got her arm in a viselike grip and wouldn't let go.

Jennifer scanned the crowd desperately. If Marilyn didn't return soon and rescue her from this creep she was going to scream.

As if in answer to her prayer, Marilyn emerged from the crowd, beaming. Her broad smile vanished when she saw Jennifer's companion. She took in the situation at a glance, her face a mask of concern, and then froze, staring over Jennifer's shoulder.

"Lee is here," she said between her teeth, trying not to let George hear what she was saying.

Jennifer attempted, without success, to disentangle herself from her unwelcome admirer. "What do you mean?" she answered, preoccupied. "Lee can't be here."

"Well, if he isn't, his clone just came through the door."

Jennifer followed the direction of Marilyn's gaze and her heart sank. Lee was making his way through the throng, accompanied by Joe Thornridge and Carl Danbury and two other players. The boys were in high good humor, out for a night on the town.

The two women stared at one another, mutually horrified.

"Let's get out of here," Jennifer hissed.

She got no argument from Marilyn, who added, "We'll slip past him; with so many people here, he'll never see you."

This plan might have worked, except for the intervention of George, who divined their intentions and started creating a ruckus, still hanging onto Jennifer for dear life.

Jennifer mentally summoned a bouncer, who of course didn't come. She concentrated on trying to shut George up and get away from him at the same time. He was amazingly strong for somebody who was almost unconscious.

"Whassa matter?" Romeo said querulously, breathing Scotch fumes in her face. "Whereya goin'?" He never relaxed his hold on her.

"Marilyn, *get somebody*," Jennifer pleaded.

Marilyn, torn between leaving Jennifer with George and summoning help, stood uncertainly, unable to act.

George crashed into a chair and overturned it, dragging Jennifer in his wake. They were attracting attention, which was the last thing Jennifer wanted. Jennifer made a last superhuman effort to break free, and succeeded only in upsetting two glasses sitting on the table. They hit the floor with a splintering of glass. She closed her eyes, and opened them to see Lee.

He was wearing a fitted body shirt in very pale lavender, almost cream, and tight black jeans. He wore a glittering gold ornament which showed at his throat, at the opening of his shirt. He looked drawn, thinner, as if he hadn't been eating or sleeping well, but it became him, as everything seemed to, making his strong cheekbones and the planes of his face more prominent.

Marilyn saw him at the same time and turned a stricken face to Jennifer.

"Hi, Jen," Lee said in a dangerously calm voice. "This guy bothering you?"

"No, no," Jennifer lied rapidly, as if George weren't fixed to her arm at that very moment, like an appendage. "Actually, we were just leaving and . . ."

At this point, the drunk stuck his jaw out pugnaciously to interrupt. "Who're you," he asked blearily. "Her father?"

"I don't think the lady wants your company, friend," Lee said. "You'd better let go of her."

Oh, God. Lee's face was acquiring the same expression she'd seen at the Heart Fund picnic, and that was not good news.

"It really doesn't matter," Jennifer babbled, trying to get between the two men. Lee stretched out one long arm and detached her from amorous George, then swept her aside like a baccarat dealer clearing the table.

"Says who?" sneered Romeo, who had obviously seen too many John Wayne movies, and was also plastered enough to disregard Lee's superior size and physical condition. He lunged wildly for Lee, who countered with a well-placed uppercut, and the fight began.

The rest of the patrons cleared a space for them, cheering them on. Several of the more enthusiastic onlookers jumped on chairs, chanting, "Fight, fight, fight." Jennifer fervently wished she could flip open a communicator and tell Spock to beam her up to the *Enterprise*. How wonderful to be able to vanish in a cloud of crystalline particles.

Marilyn's friend Jim, who appeared to be a bit slow on the uptake, slipped away from the group, and she knew he was phoning the police.

Lee, meanwhile, was having a great time. He was too much of a sportsman to take advantage of his opponent's debilitated condition, but his Marquess of Queensberry conscience did not prevent him from dancing around and jabbing at George, who swung erratically in all directions, never even coming close to his target. Jennifer saw Joe and Carl at ringside, grinning hugely, enjoying the show. She wanted to box their ears.

It wasn't long before two uniforms pushed their way through the crowd. Joe spotted them and darted forward, trying to pull Lee out of action before they reached the combatants, but to no avail. Lee shrugged his friend off like a pesky fly.

When the cops got closer, Jennifer was unpleasantly surprised to see that one of them was Harry Desautell, whom she knew from her days in private practice. She stepped behind Marilyn, trying to hide.

The police separated the two men and asked for an account of what had happened. Joe acted as spokesman, and when Jennifer's name came up, Harry looked around for her, finally spotting her peering around Marilyn like a kid playing hide and seek.

"Ms. Gardiner," Harry said in surprise. "What are you doing here? You *know* these two gladiators?"

Jennifer mumbled some inane reply, mortified.

Harry raised his eyebrows and pulled a note pad from his pocket. "Let me see here. We have disturbing the peace, inciting to riot, public drunkenness . . ."

"I'm not drunk," Lee announced from the sidelines. Harry and Jennifer turned in unison and stared at him. He shrugged and dropped his eyes.

Harry paused to squint at Lee for a moment, and then he snapped his fingers.

"Wait a minute! Aren't you that football player?"

Lee flashed his most dazzling grin and extended his hand like a candidate running for office. "That's right, officer. Lee Youngson, Philadelphia Freedom. How do you do?"

Harry shook the proferred hand, looking awed. "Oh, well, Mr. Youngson, I'd like to hear your version of what happened here."

Lee poured on his legendary charm, and by the time he was finished Officer Harry Desautell was eating out of his hand. The rookie with him was equally impressed, and Jennifer looked away, disgusted.

Harry agreed to let both men off with a warning, and the two cops got Lee's autograph before they left, escorting a partially sobered George to the door.

Lee turned to Jennifer as the crowd drifted off and things got back to normal.

"It must be nice to get away with everything because you can catch a football," Jennifer snarled.

Lee glared at her, offended. "I was trying to help you!" He held his right hand up before his face and flexed the fingers. "I think my hand is broken," he mourned, winking at Marilyn.

"I think your head is broken," Jennifer snapped.

Marilyn was watching this interchange with interest. "Aren't you going to introduce me?" she prompted Jennifer.

Jennifer waved her hand. "Marilyn, this is Lee Youngson. Lee, my friend, Marilyn Bennett."

Lee smiled charmingly. "It's a pleasure, ma'am," he drawled, doing his Montana cowboy routine. Jennifer threw him a dirty look.

Marilyn coughed. "Uh, if you'll excuse me, I think I'll go talk to Jim." She took off, tossing Jennifer a final meaningful glance as she departed.

Joe and Carl, who had remained waiting during this interval, made their presence known. "Hey, Chief, what's the holdup?" Carl whined. Joe, who had a suspicion he knew what the holdup was, kept silent, eyeing Lee and Jennifer as they conversed in low, intent voices.

"Just a minute, Carl," Lee answered, never taking his eyes from Jennifer's face. He closed the fingers of one hand around her neck, rubbing her nape with his thumb, sending a shiver down Jennifer's spine. "Let's go," he said. "I'll take you home."

Warning bells went off in Jennifer's head. "No, thank you."

Lee sighed. "Oh, come off it, Jen, what are you going to do, hang around here and wait to be accosted by George Number Two? Or spend a cozy little evening with your girl friend? I don't think she'll be leaving with you, honey; she's found more interesting company." He slid his hand down to her shoulder and turned her to face him directly. "Aren't you as lonely as I am? Isn't that what we're both doing here?"

Jennifer never had been able to lie to him. "I'll tell Marilyn," she said simply.

She saw Lee heading for Joe and Carl as she left.

Marilyn was not surprised. "I figured as much," she said. She put a hand on Jennifer's arm.

"Jen, are you sure you know what you're doing?"

Jennifer looked bleak. "No, Marilyn. I'm sure I *don't* know what I'm doing."

"That's what I thought."

"I want to go with him."

"So do I," Marilyn said, and Jennifer laughed. Marilyn always could make her see the light side of things.

"Good luck with Jim," Jennifer said.

"Thanks. Let me know what happens."

Jennifer nodded and made her way back to Lee.

It was pouring when they got outside.

"Still raining," Jennifer complained. "I haven't seen the sun for five days."

"Maybe they moved it," Lee responded, signaling for an attendant to get his car.

"It's not funny. This weather is depressing."

Lee scanned the drenched and dripping trees lining the street. "Just think how happy you'll be when it clears up. 'For truly the light is sweet, and what a pleasant thing it is for the eyes to see the sun.'"

Jennifer smiled up at him. "Yes, indeed."

He grinned back. "I hope you're impressed. My mind is a storehouse of such useless information."

"I wouldn't call that useless. Anything as beautiful as that could never be useless."

He was touched, and made light of it in response. "I know a lot of sun quotes, practically everything written about it. The sun is my totem. My father named me for his sun vision, Nitsokan, the sacred sign that makes a boy a man." He touched the gold disk at the base of his throat. "This is the Pikuni idiogram for the sun. Dawn gave it to me."

Jennifer glanced away from it. Always Dawn.

The attendant pulled up with Lee's car, and they got into it without further conversation.

Lee concentrated on driving through the downpour on the way to Jennifer's apartment and didn't speak until he pulled into Mrs. Mason's driveway.

"I'd like to come up for a while," he said quietly.

"Lee, you know that's a bad idea."

"No, I don't," he answered, turning to hold her as she reached for the handle of the door on her side.

Jennifer froze at the contact, every nerve in her body alerted.

"You see?" Lee said, at the evidence of her instant response. "It will always be like this for us."

Jennifer put her hand over her eyes. "I've known that all along, Lee, but nothing else has changed, either."

He edged closer to her, nuzzling her neck. "Please," he whispered.

How could she resist that? She relented. "All right."

They climbed the stairs in thoughtful silence, oblivious of the steadily falling rain. As soon as the door closed behind them, Lee pulled Jennifer into his arms. Chilled and damp, they clung together, famished for each other's touch.

"I don't know what I'm doing here," Lee said against her hair. "I meant not to come here again. I've never felt like this before; I simply can't stay away from you. Do you know how many times I've almost called you since the last time we were together? And then tonight when I saw you, it was all over. I had to be with you. I could no more walk away than I could fly."

Jennifer embraced him, hardly listening to the words. The warmth and the tone of his voice made the message clear.

Lee held her away from him a moment, gazing down at her. "There's a lake in Montana called Upper Saint Mary," he said. "In the spring, when the thaw from the mountains runs into it, the water turns the exact color of your eyes."

Jennifer swallowed hard. If he made another comment like that, she was going to dissolve in a puddle at his feet.

"Well, paleface," he said, searching her face, "it's your move."

Jennifer took his hand and led him down the hall to the bedroom. He followed slowly, pausing in the doorway when she snapped on the light.

"This looks like you," he said, scanning the room. "Beautiful, but practical."

"That's right," Jennifer said. "You didn't see this last time, did you? We never made it this far."

"I think we were in a bit of a hurry," he said, slipping the shawl off her shoulders, bending to kiss the bare skin thus exposed. He murmured something in his native language.

"Thank you," Jennifer said.

He chuckled. "You didn't understand what I said."

"I didn't have to."

He crushed her to him fiercely, seeking her mouth with his. Jennifer responded eagerly, on fire to fulfill his every desire. She reached back to the wall and shut off the light.

He took off her clothes, and his own, and they fell on the bed together, impatient, hungry.

Jennifer couldn't believe how much she'd missed being close to him. How was she going to bear it when this ended, as she feared it would. But Lee didn't leave her much time for thought, kissing and caressing her with steadily mounting ardor. Soon she was moving urgently against him, tracing his spine with her fingers, running her palms over the flat, hard muscles of his back. When he lowered his mouth to her breasts, she put her face against his hair, soft and smelling of herbal shampoo. She closed her eyes and wrapped her arms more tightly about him, waiting for the bliss of total union.

When it came, she arched against him, and he drew back to gaze at her from eyes dark and brilliant with feeling.

"Look at that face," he murmured. "Such a sweet face. I'll never, never forget it."

He kissed her gently on the lips, and then they gave themselves up to a world of sensation.

Afterward, they lay together quietly, Jennifer's head on Lee's shoulder. Jennifer thought he had fallen asleep, but after some minutes he got up and left her. She heard him zipping his jeans in the darkness, and the almost imperceptible sound of his footsteps going into the living room.

Jennifer waited for his return, and then realized that he wasn't coming back to the bedroom. She slipped on a robe and followed him out.

Lee was sitting on the sofa, staring into space and smoking one of the cigarettes John Ashford had left behind on the coffee table.

Jennifer halted in her tracks, astonished. "You don't smoke," she said.

Lee inhaled deeply until the tip of the cigarette glowed, and then exhaled through his nose. "I used to. I quit a long time ago when I discovered it was difficult to run when I couldn't breathe." He glanced at her, then away. "The craving returns when I'm upset or nervous." He smiled dryly. "For some strange reason, I seem to be very nervous tonight."

Jennifer bit her lip. Wonderful. Now she was driving him to revert to old, bad habits.

He saw her expression. "Oh, Jen, don't look like that," he said, stubbing out the butt and coming to take her hands, leading her to sit beside him. "I didn't mean to imply that you're responsible. You are fine, beautiful, perfect. The problem is not with you, it is with me."

"What is the problem?" Jennifer asked calmly, as if she didn't know.

"Jen, you and I, we . . . have nothing in common, we don't belong together."

Jennifer nodded slowly. "I see. Then what are you doing with me? Did I seduce you? I don't recall it, I don't make it a practice to ravish big, strong football players."

He didn't respond, not meeting her eyes.

Jennifer's anger was a defense against her pain. "I have a question for you," she said. "If you feel this way, why do you torment me by coming back?"

"You know the answer to that."

"Ah, yes, poor Nitsokan, torn between two worlds, unable to help himself, hung up on a woman who's wrong for him. Do you know that you're a hypocrite, Lee? You harbor the same prejudices against me that you once thought I had against Indians. What makes you so sure you're right about this? I have I ever asked you to do anything contrary to your background or your beliefs?"

He dropped his eyes. "Not yet," he said softly. "But one day."

Jennifer folded her trembling hands together, trying for control. "If you honestly believe that, after what we just shared in that bedroom, then I think you'd better leave."

Lee stood abruptly, thrusting his hands through his hair. "You don't understand."

"You're right," Jennifer said flatly. "I don't understand. The last time, when you left, I convinced myself that you were right. I knew what you were thinking, and I believed it, too. But now there's tonight between us, and it's becoming clearer every minute that the bottom line is either you have faith in me, or you don't. And you obviously don't."

Lee turned on her, his eyes blazing the way they

had when he'd spoken of his sister. "You have no idea what you're talking about!" he said bitterly. He jabbed his thumb at his bare chest. "Look at me. Do you think because I went to college, talk like an accountant, wear these clothes, that I am *like* you? What did you expect, war paint and sign language? What you see is a survival suit, protective coloration. Don't be fooled by it. Underneath I am as red as Montana clay."

His voice was hoarse, his features contorted. "I am Siksika, Nitsokan, Youngest Son." His hands stabbed the air, the right rubbing the left, back and forth twice, making the sign for "Indian" he'd once showed her, followed by another she didn't understand. "I am Indian, and I am not like you."

Gone was the light tone of the early days, when he had joked about Chingachgook. This was no laughing matter now. He saw a threat to his basic identity in his strong feeling for Jennifer and was asserting himself in the most fundamental way: "I am Indian, and I am not like you."

They stood facing each other, emotional, spent. Jennifer felt the rejection and struck back with her best weapon, words.

"Funny how these scruples always arise *after* you've slept with me," she said nastily. "They never seem to bother you before."

He flinched, as if she'd struck him. "That's a cheap shot, Jen, unworthy of you. I don't deserve it."

Jennifer put her hand to her mouth, choking back a sob. She would not cry in front of him.

"You'll have to forgive me," she said. "I'm hurt and confused and somewhat lacking in tact this evening."

Lee studied her face, his own unreadable. "I'm sorry I hurt you, paleface. I never meant to."

"Just go, will you please go?"

She didn't watch him go back to the bedroom for the rest of his things and didn't turn when she heard him pause behind her.

"Jen, I—" he began.

"Leave. Now."

He did so, and she waited for the sound of his motor to fade away outside before she gave way to the tears she'd held in check so carefully.

Good-bye, Nitsokan.

8

∞∞∞∞∞∞∞∞

Jennifer made herself sick over the whole thing. She threw up her breakfast two mornings running and was so tired she could barely keep awake. To make matters worse, she was overdue for her period, and felt bloated and out of sorts. She called in sick to work for several days and spent her time at home sleeping and feeling sorry for herself.

Dolores kept her posted on what was happening with daily telephone calls and startled her by concluding one conversation with the bulletin that Lee was ill also.

"What's the matter with him?" Jennifer asked, alarmed.

"He has the chicken pox."

Jennifer laughed so hard she dropped the phone. Dolores' voice came tinnily through the receiver. "Jen? You still there?"

Jennifer picked the receiver up again, wiping her eyes. "Yes, I'm still here. Are you sure about that story?"

"Sure as sunrise. They think he caught it during that visit to the children's hospital with you. You'll probably be next."

"No fear. I had it in second grade. Whatever I've got, that isn't it. How long will he be off the roster?"

"Two weeks or so. Roy says he's mad as hell.

Everybody else thinks it's hilarious. So do you, I gather."

"Funniest thing I've heard in a long time."

There was a pause. "What's going on with you and Lee?"

"Nothing." At the moment, that was true.

"Hmmm. A likely story. Well, I won't keep you. Rest up and take care of yourself, I'll call you tomorrow. Bye-bye."

"Bye." Jennifer hung up, still chuckling. She went to her bedroom to turn on the radio, and glanced at the pillows where Lee's head had rested. Her resentment of him faded with each passing day, leaving only the love behind. He couldn't help how he felt, and his convictions were hurting him as well as Jennifer. No one would ever be as good for him or love him as much as Jennifer did. And he would never want anyone the way he wanted her. Jennifer knew that on some subconscious level he was well aware of all this, and he would have to live with the choice he had made for the rest of his life.

She lay down on the bed and took another nap.

Jennifer was back at work a week when Dolores buzzed her on the intercom one afternoon.

"Dawn Blacktree to see you," Dolores said.

Jennifer put aside the work she was doing, puzzled. What was this? She had sent Lee a funny get well card, but had not expected a reply and so far had received none. Could this visit be connected to that impulsive act? Was Dawn here to tell her that Lee wanted no further communication between them?

"Send her in," she told Dolores.

Dolores opened the door, eyeing Jennifer cautiously. She lingered as long as was decently possible and then went out quietly, closing the door. Jennifer wasn't fooled. She was probably standing on the other side with a glass to her ear.

Dawn was looking very lovely, dressed in a deep rose pantsuit, her glorious hair falling straight to her waist from a center part. She seated herself gracefully in a conference chair and gazed serenely at Jennifer.

"Hello, Dawn. It's nice to see you again. What can I do for you?"

"Lee asked me to come in to see you. Our local newspaper in Montana needs copies of some of his publicity releases. They're preparing a Lee Youngson Day back home, a sort of a county fair, and the proceeds from the booths and exhibits will go to the Indian school Lee and I attended. This is a list of the publications and the dates."

Jennifer took the sheet of paper Dawn handed her, aware that Lee had sent Dawn to do this rather than call Jennifer himself.

"I'll have duplicates prepared today and mail them to Lee's house."

"Thank you." Dawn smoothed her tunic over her knees. "That is not the only reason I came, Ms. Gardiner."

"Please call me Jennifer."

"All right, Jennifer. I could have telephoned, but I wanted to see you in person."

Jennifer waited, watching the Indian girl.

"Lee has been ill," Dawn began.

"Yes, I heard that. I hope he's feeling better now."

Dawn met Jennifer's eyes directly, her black gaze candid. "His illness has been of the spirit as well as the body."

"I . . . don't know what you mean."

Dawn smiled gently. "I think you do."

Jennifer said nothing, listening.

"Nitsokan . . . admires you very much," Dawn said, reverting to the use of Lee's Pikuni name, choosing her words carefully. "He is most unhappy right now."

"I am sorry to hear that."

Dawn's eyes were wise. "You are an intelligent woman, Jennifer. You say the correct, polite thing, but you are thinking all the while, your mind racing as you make pleasant conversation."

"Dawn—"

Dawn held up her hand. "Please let me finish. You did not know Nitsokan as a child, as I did. I was younger, yes, but I saw a great deal with the clarity of a child's vision. You do not know what his life was like. He was taken away from us to play football, and he has been straddling two worlds ever since, not completely at home in either one. For a man of his strong loyalties, deep commitments, it is very difficult."

"I can appreciate that."

Dawn smiled again. "Can you? I think not."

Jennifer was tired of being lectured about her lack of perception. "I am not completely without understanding, Dawn."

Dawn folded her hands in her lap. "I see that you resent me, because you think I am his lover. I am not. I wish to be, and his wife also, but he does not love me. I think he *wants* to, but he does not."

Jennifer was stunned into silence. That was quite an admission.

"You look surprised," Dawn said.

"I am. I don't understand why you're telling me this."

"To help you," Dawn said simply. "I know how hard it is to care for Nitsokan. Others have come and gone, attracted perhaps by the money and the glamour, what he calls 'the image,' but I sense these things mean little to you. If you were like the rest, he would not think so much of you. He has not told me this, but I have guessed. He would be very angry if he knew I was talking to you this way, but because of his regard for you, I have done so."

Jennifer didn't know what to say. Such generosity to a person Dawn could only view as a rival was very rare.

"I must go," Dawn said, rising.

Jennifer walked her to the elevator. As the doors opened, she put a hand on Dawn's arm.

"I hope he does find happiness, Dawn."

Dawn smiled sadly. "For Nitsokan, it will not be easy. Like the sun which is his totem, he burns brightly, but with a dangerous light." She inclined her head in farewell as the doors closed in front of her.

Jennifer stood staring at the space Dawn had occupied seconds before. The Blackfoot girl's innate dignity and quiet self-containment had made her feel inadequate, outclassed. She shook off the notion and turned to go back to her office, colliding with Dolores.

"What?" Dolores demanded. "What?"

"You're stuttering, Dolores."

"Why did she come here?"

"She wanted copies of some of Lee's releases. No big deal."

"Then why did you look like that when you came out of your office with her?"

"Like what?"

"Like she had dropped a bomb on you."

"Your ever-exotic imagination is working overtime again, Dolores."

"Don't give me that. If you would only—"

"Do you *like* your job here, Dolores?" Jennifer interrupted pointedly.

"Boy, are you a grouch."

"I seem to recall telling you that a memo had to be hand delivered to the city editor at the *Inquirer* by four o'clock. To my knowledge, you haven't left yet."

Dolores took her jacket from the back of her chair and picked up the envelope from her desk. "I'm gone," she said. "But I hope your disposition has improved by the time I get back."

Her boss reflected glumly that there wasn't much chance of that.

Jennifer realized that she was pregnant on a gorgeous October day at 8:30 in the morning. She had struggled to button her blouse, and when her skirt wouldn't zip, she gave up in frustration, reaching for a looser pair of slacks instead. What on earth had she been eating to cause this? She'd been too nauseated lately to really . . .

Her hand froze in the act of reaching into the closet, and she slowly sank to the edge of the bed. She'd missed a period, but had thought that was caused by her bout with what she'd assumed was the flu. Until now she hadn't connected the frequent upset stomachs, the fatigue, the general malaise with the first, and most important, clue. She sat for a few moments, thinking, and then took off her remaining clothes and examined herself in the full-length mirror.

There was no doubt about it. Her breasts were fuller and her usually flat stomach looked rounder, more pronounced. The difference was slight, but noticeable if you looked for it.

She raced to the kitchen, stark naked, and ripped the calendar off the wall. Her breath coming in excited gasps, she counted off the days, and then dropped it on the table, a look of wonder on her face. It was true.

Jennifer called her gynecologist and made an appointment for the following week. Then she called her office and said that she would be late. This was too much to absorb in a few minutes. If she tried to drive to work now, she would probably wind up in a wreck.

Jennifer's first reaction was a surge of pure, unadulterated joy. Lee's baby. She was going to have Lee's baby.

Not for a moment did she consider the alternative. She wanted to be a mother, and a mother to this child in particular.

A curious calmness descended over her after the initial burst of emotion. Jennifer knew exactly what she would do. She would find another job, move away, and raise the child by herself.

Telling Lee was out of the question. His strong sense of duty would compel him to marry her, and she didn't need a shotgun husband. If he hadn't wanted her enough to take the step before, she would not use this as an added inducement.

Jennifer got up and headed for the bedroom to dress again, grinning to herself. Lee's baby! Maybe it

would look like him, have his smile, his easy, effortless grace. She sagged against the wall, laughing out
loud. What a gas.

Jennifer was waiting for Marilyn when she got
home from work, toting a sack of groceries and Jeff's
bookbag and lunchbox. Jeff was spending the night
with a friend, and had sent the day's debris home
with Mom.

"Hi, Jen," Marilyn said, as she unlocked her door
and staggered inside. "What are you doing here?"

"I need your advice."

"What, again? Cawassa's favorite son up to his old
tricks? Come on in, just let me dump this stuff."

Marilyn set her bundles down on the kitchen table
and kept walking, finally collapsing in a living room
chair. "Well?"

"I think I'm pregnant."

Marilyn got up again instantly, raising her hand to
forestall further discussion. "Don't say anything else,
I beg of you. I need a drink before I hear the rest of
this." She got a bottle and a shot glass from the dry
sink in the corner and bolted two fingers before
looking at Jennifer again.

"Would you mind repeating that, please?"

"You heard me the first time."

"You *think* you're pregnant. Don't you *know*?"

"Well, I'm new at this, Marilyn, I've never been
pregnant before. I don't know how I'm supposed to
feel. But I'm pretty sure, and I'm going to Dr. Bellini
next Wednesday."

Marilyn closed her eyes. "Jennifer, what is wrong
with you? How could you be so irresponsible?"

"Don't scold me, Marilyn. I've been thinking."

"I certainly hope so."

"I'm going to have it."

Marilyn set her glass down with a bang. "Now I've heard everything. Do you realize what you'd be taking on? Raising a child is a full-time, lifelong responsibility. I've done it alone for years and I know what I'm talking about."

"That's exactly my point," Jennifer replied. "You've done it, so can I. Marilyn, you have a child by a man you loved. You are reminded of him every time you look at Jeff and remember that love. I want that, too, and this is my chance to have it."

Marilyn fell silent, running the tip of her finger along the rim of her glass. "I suppose you won't consider telling Lee."

"You suppose correctly."

"Don't you think he'll figure it out when he returns next season to see you packing a papoose that will probably bear a startling resemblance to his family?"

"I have a plan to cover that," Jennifer said. "And in case you get any ideas about telling him yourself, be warned that I will put a contract out on you the minute I hear about it."

Marilyn sighed. "What's your plan?"

Jennifer outlined what she was going to do, while Marilyn went to the kitchen and made grilled cheese sandwiches. They conversed through the alcove between the two rooms, until Marilyn carried the food in on a tray.

Marilyn handed Jennifer a plate and said, "Let me know what I can do to help. I'll miss you. I have some money saved, if you need it."

Jennifer smiled. "For heaven's sake, Marilyn,

you're acting like I'm going to wind up slinging hash in some roadside diner, scrubbing floors at night to buy junior's little booties. I'm a professional, I'll make enough money to support both of us. And there are plenty of day-care centers and nursery schools to enable me to continue working. So stop worrying and be happy for me."

"Here's to motherhood," Marilyn said, saluting Jennifer with her sandwich. "I withdraw my objections."

Jennifer reciprocated and then took a huge bite.

On Monday morning Jennifer called two firms of "headhunters" in New York, personnel agencies that placed people in her field. She told them what kind of position she wanted and the same day mailed out the resumés she had typed up over the weekend. She felt capable, efficient, resolved. She had time yet, and it was likely she would find something suitable before her appearance gave away her condition.

The last thing she had to do, before tendering her resignation, which would have to wait until she had an offer, was to tell Dolores what she was planning. In the interest of fairness, Dolores should know that she might shortly be working for a new boss.

Jennifer waited until Dolores was getting ready to leave for the day, and then asked her to sit down for a minute.

"I have some news, Dolores."

"You're pregnant."

Jennifer stared at her, stunned. "How did you know?"

"A blind man could see it."

"I didn't realize it was so obvious."

Dolores crossed her legs. "Relax. It isn't obvious, only to me. I work with you every day, remember?" She swung one foot in 3/4 time. "And I saw you throwing up in the ladies' room on several occasions."

So much for privacy at the office. "I'm going to move, Dolores. I'm looking for another job."

"It's Lee Youngson's, isn't it?"

Jennifer didn't answer.

"Ah, come on, Jen, who do you think you're kidding? After that dance at the Stratford, your mutual fascination is hardly a secret."

"That's exactly the reason I have to go."

"You're going to have it, then."

"Yes."

"Good for you."

Jennifer felt a wave of affection for her secretary. She wasn't going to try to talk Jennifer out of it. She understood.

Dolores stood up. "Now let me see. It's time to start taking care of you around here. Glasses of milk on coffee break, feet up for ten minutes in the PM, no salt, no booze, easy on the calories. I'm at your service. All I ask in return is that you name it after me."

Jennifer laughed. "You missed your calling, Dolores. You should be running a prenatal clinic."

"I will be, right here."

"Not a word of this to anybody."

"My lips are sealed."

They packed up and left together, united in their shared secret.

* * *

Jennifer kept her doctor's appointment, and the nurse called her two days later with the results of her tests. They were positive. Jennifer was indeed pregnant.

That Saturday Jennifer took the train to New York for her first interview.

9

Autumn came to eastern Pennsylvania. The leaves on the trees turned a myriad of colors, and summer transformed itself to fall. The football season was in full swing, and Jennifer kept track of Lee's progress by reading what came across her desk and watching the sports coverage on the local news.

She missed him more than she would have believed possible. Nights alone were agony, so she filled them with packing as much as she could ahead of time. She wasn't sure where she was going, but she was sure she was going to go.

Almost every Saturday she interviewed for jobs. After a preliminary meeting during which she conferred with the placement agency's representative, she was presented with a description of open positions as they became available. Since she was willing to go anywhere and also to take a cut in salary, these were more numerous than she had expected. If she and the prospective employer were both interested, the agency set up a meeting. Twice she flew out-of-town, but most often she was interviewed by someone from the company who happened to be in Philadelphia or New York.

The schedule was exhausting. Jennifer was beginning to feel better, the nausea had almost disappeared, but she spent most Saturdays dressing up, trying to make a good impression on strangers, and

trekking back and forth to and from hotel suites or
luncheon appointments. On Sundays, she crashed.
She almost relished the constant activity, however. It
didn't give her much time to think about other things.

Thanksgiving was almost upon her before she
found the job she wanted. She was beginning to
think she never would, but just when she was giving
up, the placement representative contacted her with
the ideal position. It was similar to the one she
presently had, but with much wider ranging responsi-
bilities, for less money, with the Tampa Bay Bengals,
in Florida. Travel and moving expenses would be
paid as part of the package. She met with the
personnel vice-president in New York and accepted
the offer the same day it was made.

Her next task was composing a letter of resignation for Harold Salamone. By the time she finished,
her living room was littered with scrap paper.
Dolores typed it the next day, and Jennifer asked for
an appointment to see him.

He was shocked and tried to talk her out of her
decision. Jennifer was adamant but understood his
puzzlement. Her statement that the reason for her
move was "personal" hardly explained her actions.
He insisted that she contact him if she ever needed
work in the future, and she promised that she would.

The Saturday before Thanksgiving Jennifer tuned
in to the Freedom's home game from force of habit.
It was not televised in the local area, so she listened
to it on the radio. There was some small comfort in
hearing Lee's exploits described. She couldn't help
feeling a certain pride in his accomplishments. She
was sorting dishes for the moving company to wrap
and pack, washing the ones she was planning to
take, and putting the rest in a box for storage.

The announcer was describing a pass from Joe Thornridge to Lee when he suddenly broke off, and then resumed with a strong undercurrent of repressed excitement in his voice.

"Lee Youngson is down, hit hard by number 31, Melvin Banks. Youngson was reaching for that Thornridge pass when he was tackled by the 6'4" 250-pound Banks, and you can bet Lee must be smarting from that one, folks."

Jennifer paused, alerted.

"Lee Youngson is hurt!" the announcer caroled. "He is motionless on the ground, and the officials are calling for a stretcher. No way to tell the extent of his injuries, of course, but he appears to be unconscious and is about to be carried off the field."

The dishtowel Jennifer was holding slipped from her fingers and fell to the floor.

"The word here in the booth is that an ambulance is on the way to take the injured man directly to Center City Hospital. To repeat, Lee Youngson is being carried, unconscious, off the field and is being taken to—"

Jennifer snapped off the radio with trembling fingers. Mechanically, she went to the closet and got her coat, then picked up her purse and keys.

Her only thought was to get to Lee as soon as possible.

Jennifer remembered nothing of the drive to the hospital. She obeyed traffic signals and negotiated city streets in a daze. She wasn't sure she could get in to see Lee when she arrived, but she knew she had to try.

There was a crush of reporters in the lobby of the hospital, and she pushed past them impatiently. A hospital spokesman was dealing with them, handing out the usual party line about "resting comfortably" and "everything possible being done." Jennifer knew the truth was to be found elsewhere.

But she soon discovered that no one would tell her anything. She wasn't a member of the family, or part of the team's staff, and she couldn't even find out what floor Lee was on. She was standing in the reception area, terrified, frustrated, when she saw Joe Thornridge speeding in a side door, dodging the press, his face hunched into his collar. They were listening to the administrator and didn't see him.

Jennifer wanted to shout for him but feared attracting attention. She waited until he had turned down one of the corridors and then scurried after him as fast as she could.

He jumped when she grabbed his arm, whirling to face her.

"Joe, it's me."

His eyes widened. "Jenny! Why'd you pounce on me like that?"

"I didn't want the reporters to see you. How is he?"

Joe's plain face darkened with concern. "Not good, sugar, not good. He's still out, and these doctors here can't seem to figger why."

The knot forming in Jennifer's stomach tightened another notch. "What happened?" she asked.

"I screwed up, is what happened," Joe said miserably. "I overshot him by a mile, but you know he's always got to try for 'em, even if they're twenty feet over his head. Banks never woulda been able to nail him like that if he hadn't been reachin' for the moon."

"Where is he?"

"Third floor. Intensive care."

"Intensive care?" Jennifer repeated faintly. Suddenly she didn't feel very well. She stopped abruptly and put her hand to her throat. Air seemed to be in short supply.

Joe put his arm around her and steadied her against his side. "Hey, hey, li'l lady, take it easy." He turned her to face him and put his hands on her shoulders, looking down at her. He didn't say anything for a few seconds, just studied her expression. Then he stepped back and took her hand. "C'mon, sugar," he said quietly. "We'll go up and see what the story is."

The ride on the elevator seemed endless. Jennifer clutched Joe's hand as if it were a life preserver.

The scene outside intensive care was grim. Roy O'Grady and Coach Rankin sat on one of the visitors' benches, furiously puffing cigarettes and whispering. They reminded Jennifer of French films from the sixties in which everyone smoked constantly and conversed in low, intent voices through a carcinogenic cloud. Dawn sat apart from them, her customary composure undisturbed, watching Jennifer's approach calmly. Carl Danbury and his wife, a statuesque beauty with a curly Afro, stood off to one side. They didn't look happy.

Mrs. Danbury took one look at Jennifer and said to Joe, "Get this woman a glass of water."

Joe obliged, walking to a water cooler at the end of the hall, and Mrs. Danbury extended her hand. "You must be Jennifer. My husband told me about you. I'm Rita Danbury."

Jennifer shook hands, wondering what Carl had said.

Mrs. Danbury led her to a seat next to Dawn and

then sat herself, putting Jennifer in the middle between the two other women. Joe came back and silently handed Jennifer her drink.

"Did you call Sal Barbetti back?" Rita asked him. Joe nodded.

"Is that the man who owns the restaurant?" Jennifer asked.

Joe nodded again.

"When I was there with Lee, he said something about a favor Lee did for his son. Do you know what that was?"

"Oh, his kid got into some trouble with the police when he was out to see his cousin Angelo. Lee vouched for the kid to the cops, took him in to live with him while the kid was on probation, saved him from a juvenile home, certain. Sal would do anythin' for Lee."

So would I, Jennifer thought, but that isn't helping right now.

A doctor emerged from the private room, and everybody stood. He shook his head. "I'm sorry. He's still unconscious."

Everybody sat down again, dispiritedly. Rita Danbury patted Jennifer's knee.

Dawn spoke up. "May I see him, Doctor?"

The doctor nodded. "Just for a minute," he said. "Since you're family."

Jennifer turned to her, surprised.

Dawn met her glance. "I am a distant cousin," she said. "But since the rest of Lee's relatives are in Montana, I am taking responsibility." She followed the doctor into the room.

Jennifer put her head back against the wall and closed her eyes.

When Dawn came out again after a short interval

she said, "Would you let this young lady see him, please?" She indicated Jennifer. "Miss Gardiner is a close friend of Lee's, and I would appreciate it."

The doctor hesitated, and then agreed, reluctantly. "All right. But be quick about it."

Jennifer pressed Dawn's hand for a moment in gratitude and walked past the doctor into the antiseptic cubicle.

She paused at the foot of the bed, as the doctor gently pulled the door closed. At first glance Lee looked asleep, but closer examination revealed an unhealthy pallor beneath his coppery skin. His black hair was like an ink stain against the stark whiteness of the pillow. Traces of the blackout he had worn during the game remained under his eyes, making the sockets appear hollowed and sunken. His big hands, which could play Chopin, catch a football from any angle, and make love to Jennifer so expertly, lay curled on the sheet, relaxed and lifeless.

Jennifer stood looking for a few moments, and then went to the side of the bed, pushing back the lock of hair that always fell across his forehead.

"I love you," she said, because she knew he couldn't hear it. "Please wake up, and get well."

Then she marched out of the room and down the hall to the lounge, pushing through the swinging door and walking straight to the window overlooking the parking lot. She cried silently, wiping her tears with the back of her hand.

She turned at a slight sound behind her. Joe was standing against the wall, his hands in his pockets, watching her. He held out his arms, and she ran into them.

"Oh, Joe," Jennifer sobbed, "he isn't going to *die*, is he?"

"No, no," Joe murmured soothingly, rubbing her back as if he were burping a baby. "Course not, course not. Need more'n a li'l ol' bump on the head to take that Injun out." Joe's drawl was becoming more pronounced as the evening wore on. But it came and went, like the tide.

"But he looks so . . . . still," Jennifer said.

"Why, sure he does. That's just because you're not used to seein' him stayin' in one position that long. He's always runnin' aroun' like his tail was on fire, and so now the comparison is scary, that's all." He pushed her hair out of her face and said, "C'mon back, now, with the others. You shouldn't be alone in here."

Jennifer followed him slowly back to the group.

They kept vigil all night long. Rita Danbury went out for coffee at about 3 A.M., and Joe called his wife twice, for moral support, since there was nothing to report. Jennifer fell asleep for an hour huddled under Carl's coat and had just awakened when a nurse came out of Lee's room, grinning from ear to ear. All eyes turned to her, and she pointed to the intern behind her, who announced smilingly, "He just regained consciousness for a few seconds."

Carl punched Joe on the shoulder. Rita gestured to the rising sun through the window, and said, "Amen. Joy cometh in the morning."

"What did he say?" Jennifer asked.

The intern rolled his eyes. "He said, 'Am I in a hospital?' I told him that he was, and he said, 'Get me out of here.' "

Carl burst out laughing. "Sounds like our boy is on the road to recovery," he said.

The doctor held up a hand. "Well, he's not out of

the woods yet by a long shot, but it's a very good sign. My guess is that he'll be with us for a while; we'll have to run quite a few tests to make sure there was no damage before we can let him play again." He surveyed the bedraggled company. "I suggest all you good people go home. I have your number, Miss Blacktree, and I'll call you if there's any change. You can visit him during the regularly scheduled hours."

Buoyed by relief, the group began to assemble personal belongings in preparation for departure. Joe put his arm around Jennifer.

"Why don't you come home with me?" he said. "My wife will make breakfast for us; you'll feel better."

Jennifer shook her head. "I'm fine, Joe. I just want to go home and get some sleep."

Joe nodded. "All right." He hesitated. "Jen, I . . ." He stopped and sighed. "He's the stubbornest cuss I ever met. Why is it that he can't see . . ."

Jennifer interrupted him. "We're both dead tired, Joe. I don't think we should talk about this now."

He looked mulish. "Not now. But sometime. I mean it, this is not my last word on the subject."

Yes, it is, Joe, Jennifer thought. I won't be around to hear any more.

Jennifer stopped on her way out to thank Dawn. "It was kind of you to think of me, to let me see him," she said to the Indian girl. "Isn't it wonderful that he came out of it?"

"Just as the sun rose," Dawn said. "It was the power of his totem."

"Take care of him," Jennifer said.

Dawn did not miss the finality of Jennifer's words. "You will not be back to visit him?"

"No."

"Shall I tell him anything for you?"

"No."

Dawn inclined her head, accepting Jennifer's decision.

Jennifer walked out to her car, buttoning her jacket against the chill of the crisp November morning.

Jennifer spent Thanksgiving with her father and his wife, breaking the news of her move to Florida. She said nothing of the coming baby, considering it best to let him absorb the shocks in small doses. He seemed concerned, but apparently regarded the relocation as a career choice, and Jennifer let him think that. He was too busy riding herd on his three teen-age stepchildren to worry about it much anyway.

She had previously contacted a real estate agency that handled rentals in the Tampa area, and the day after Thanksgiving she flew to Florida to look for an apartment. A very patient agent spent a long time with her, and she finally found something close to the Bengals' office that was in good repair and that she could afford. It was still occupied, but Jennifer was promised it would be vacant by the time she needed it. She flew back to Philadelphia tired but satisfied with her efficiency. She was handling everything very well.

Her last few days with the Freedom were occupied with putting things in order for her departure, and saying good-bye to everyone, especially Dolores, who was proving to be very emotional. After promising hourly that she would write and telephone whenever she could, she heard herself inviting Dolores down over the Christmas holidays. This finally placated her, and she concentrated on helping Jennifer get ready to go.

Lee was still in the hospital. Joe kept her posted on his condition, which was steadily improving, but he wasn't ready for discharge yet. They were keeping him there for "observation," whatever that meant, but he was ambulatory and demanding to be released. Jennifer said nothing to Joe of her impending move; she would be gone before he realized it, as he was still playing and busy with the team.

Jennifer decided to take her car with her and drive down, rather than sell it and buy another when she got there. Marilyn helped her load it with a few final things after the movers had left, and she and Mrs. Mason took turns crying and warning her about the hazards of a woman traveling such a distance alone.

Jennifer was worn out by the time she finally got on the road. She had planned what stops she would make and telephoned ahead for reservations, but Marilyn and Mrs. Mason had convinced her that disaster awaited at every turn. Twin Cassandras, prophesying doom, they had set the tone for the trip, and Jennifer couldn't shake off the feeling that they knew something she didn't. She pulled onto the interstate with a heavy heart.

The move to Florida was a nightmare from start to finish. Jennifer promised herself that when, or if, she recovered from it she was going to set her two friends up in the fortune-telling business. They would all make a mint.

Her car broke down in Georgia in some tiny hamlet with one service station, and it took her two days to get it fixed. She spent her time reading magazines purchased at the general store. They were several months out of date and on subjects that did not fascinate. When she started on *Popular Mechanics* for the second time, she knew she was in trouble. To make matters worse, she hadn't been able to reach the Holiday Inn where she had reserved a room and so she had to stay at a dilapidated "rooming house" inhabited by a bunch of escapees from the Li'l Abner comic strip. They overcharged her shamelessly at the service station, but she paid the price gladly in order to get going once more.

She thought she had it made when she hit Florida, but discovered that she was wrong again. She got lost. She hadn't realized before that everything in central Florida looks like everything else in central Florida. Nothing but citrus groves and trailer parks for endless miles on either side of a straight ribbon of sandy, dusty road. When she at last got directions she could understand from a state trooper, she had wasted almost a day wandering aimlessly among the orange trees.

She drove into Tampa at night, and its lights and beautiful bay looked like the Promised Land to her. But not for long. When she called the real estate agency in the morning, she was told that her apartment was not empty yet—there had been a slight delay. And as there was no place for the movers to put her furniture, it went into storage in the company's warehouse in Spring Hill, an hour's drive away. And, oh yes, there would be a slight storage charge.

A few days before she was to start her new job, Jennifer found herself at a coffee shop making a mental list of everybody she was going to sue and abusing Lee Youngson and his descendants for three generations, one of whom she was carrying in her belly. The restaurant was filled with itinerant truck drivers and farm workers who called to each other in indecipherable Southern accents and wiped faces perspiring from the seventy-five-degree weather and eighty percent humidity. Jennifer felt that she had been transported to another country, so foreign did the environment seem. And when the waitress yo-deled after her, "Y'all come back now, heah?" her throat tightened with unshed tears. My God, she even missed Joe Thornridge.

She took possession of her apartment that after-noon and got the moving company to deliver her things. She collapsed that night and slept on the floor, using a tablecloth for a blanket.

The next morning, she read in the Tampa newspa-per that Lee had been discharged from the hospital.

10

〜◦◦◦◦◦◦◦◦◦◦〜

Jennifer was in the middle of stacking books on the bottom shelf of a wicker étagère when the doorbell rang. Sighing, she dusted her palms on her jeans and got off her knees, swiping ineffectually at the wisps of hair that fell around her face. After a full day of unpacking, she was really in no condition to greet anyone. But it was probably just another of her new neighbors stopping by with a cake. Two were already sitting on the kitchen table. Marveling at the miracle of Southern hospitality, she pulled open the door of the apartment with a manufactured smile.

It vanished very quickly. Bradley Youngson stood in the hall.

Jennifer's heart began to pound. She tugged at her shirttails to make sure they covered her burgeoning midsection and whispered, "How did you find me?"

His dark eyes never left her face. "Simple," he said. "I went to your old office and threatened Dolores with every form of mayhem known to man, and a few I invented, if she didn't tell me where you were."

Jennifer closed her eyes. Damn Dolores and her big mouth. If she had told Lee that Jennifer was pregnant, Jennifer was going to take the first plane back to Philly and tie her to the Penn Central tracks.

They surveyed each other in silence. Lee looked wonderful, as usual, immaculate in designer jeans and a white turtleneck sweater that flattered his dusky skin. By contrast, Jennifer, exhausted and filthy, felt like the television illustration for a person with an Excedrin headache.

"May I come in?" he asked pointedly.

Her mind whirling with a dozen questions, Jennifer stepped aside just as her newly installed telephone began to ring. "Excuse me," she said.

What now? Jennifer thought as she moved to answer it. Lee stood in the middle of the room, looking around. There wasn't much to see except piles of cardboard boxes and general confusion.

It was Dolores. "Oh, Jenny, I'm so glad I finally got you. I've been trying for two days, but you didn't have a number. Lee Youngson was here, he made me tell him where you were, and I'm afraid he'll—"

"You're a little late, Dolores," Jennifer interrupted her. "He's standing in my living room."

Jennifer eyed Lee who was staring, mystified, at the poster Jennifer had tacked to the wall. It was the Middle English version of the Prologue to Chaucer's *Canterbury Tales,* a departing gift from Mrs. Mason.

Dolores groaned. "Oh, God, I was afraid of that. Jennifer, please forgive me, but he was so upset, I thought he was going to kill me."

"It's all right, Dolores," Jennifer said wearily. "It doesn't matter."

Strangely enough, it didn't. Everything else had gone wrong; having Lee show up to find her looking like an underage bag lady was just another calamity to add to a long list.

"I didn't tell him you were pregnant," Dolores said

piously. There was a pause. "Though if I were you,
I—"

"*Thank you,* Dolores," Jennifer said in a strong
voice. "It was thoughtful of you to call. I'll be in
touch. Good-bye." She dropped the receiver back
into its cradle.

"I take it that was Dolores," Lee said.

"Yes."

"Calling to warn you of the impending arrival of
the rampaging savage," he added.

Jennifer said nothing.

"Oh, well, I'm glad to see she survived her last
encounter with me. She was looking strangely pale
when I left; I fear I've lost a fan." He jerked his
thumb over his shoulder at the wall. "What is that?
German?"

"The Prologue to Chaucer's *Canterbury Tales* in
the original Middle English. It looks and sounds
like German. Old English does, too, only more
so."

He nodded, watching her. "I wondered why it
seemed familiar."

Jennifer met his eyes, asking herself why she was
babbling about Chaucer when she wanted to fling
herself on Lee and kiss him until he couldn't breathe.
But he mustn't know that. She crossed her arms on
her stomach, concealing it from his sharp eyes.

"Why are you here?" she asked.

He shook his head. "Don't beat around the bush,
Jennifer," he said sarcastically. "Come directly to the
point."

She waited, unmoving.

Lee propped one foot, encased in a leather top-
sider, on an overturned box and leaned forward with
his arms folded on his upraised knee. "I've been

accepted to medical school. I'm retiring from football and starting at Temple University in the fall."

Jennifer felt the sting of tears behind her eyes. He had done it. He had really done it. Her throat closed with emotion.

"That's wonderful, Lee," she managed to get out. "Congratulations."

His black eyes bored into hers. "You're responsible, you know. You convinced me to try. Without your encouragement, I never would have had the nerve."

Jennifer turned away, biting her lip hard to hold back the tears. "Nonsense," she said in an approximation of a normal tone. "You would have come to the same realization of what you wanted sooner or later; I just brought it into the open faster, that's all."

There was no reply from the man behind her. "Is that what you came to tell me?" she asked, coughing slightly to disguise the hoarseness of her voice. That couldn't be all. He had bludgeoned Dolores, tracked her down like Sherlock Holmes, and flown thousands of miles to deliver *this* message? He could have telephoned or written. She was puzzled.

"Well, yes " he said, sounding confused. Then she was suddenly seized by the shoulders and hauled around to face him.

"Goddamnit," he said between gritted teeth, "why do I always allow you to do this to me? That wasn't what I came to say at all." He stared down at her, his stark features filled with emotion.

"Why did you leave your job with the Freedom?" he demanded.

"I wanted a change of scenery, warmer weather," Jennifer said evasively. "What business is it of yours?"

"I'll tell you what business of mine it is," Lee said grimly. "I think you left because of me."

"Don't flatter yourself," Jennifer said, trying to shrug free of his viselike grip.

"I think you wanted to be gone before I reported back to camp next fall. You didn't know I would be starting school, and you resigned so as not to see me again," he continued as if she hadn't spoken.

"You think I would give up a job I worked years to get just to avoid a few uncomfortable moments with you?" she said scornfully. "I've heard of giant egos, but yours must be the size of an airplane hangar."

"That's not the reason," he said calmly, holding her fast despite her fruitless efforts to wriggle free. "You gave up the job because you're in love with me and you couldn't stand to be around me and not have me."

Jennifer stared at him, dumbfounded.

His beautiful eyes became lambent and full of feeling. "At least, I hope so, because I came here to tell you I love you and want to take you back with me."

The silence was deafening.

"I said I love you," Lee repeated. "Do you love me?" It was issued like a challenge.

No response.

Lee shook her gently. "Aren't you speaking English today?"

Jennifer burst into tears.

Lee sighed and released her. "Look, something is wrong here. When I say I love you, you're supposed to say 'I love you, too' and smother me in an ardent embrace."

Jennifer sat on an orange crate and bawled.

"Oh, fine," Lee said, throwing up his hands. "What am I supposed to derive from this?"

When she continued to cry, he sat down next to her and waited for the storm to pass, surveying her with an expression of mixed exasperation and tenderness. As she subsided to an occasional sniffle, he said, "Does that mean you love me, or not?"

Jennifer wiped her nose on her sleeve. "Of course I love you, you jackass."

She didn't see his long, deep, silent sigh of relief. In a voice that was not quite steady he said, "I see. Don't you think it would be more appropriate to say, 'Of course I love you, my darling'? 'You jackass' hardly seems the proper form of address."

She looked up at him from under long, spiky lashes matted with tears. "Are you going to pick a fight about that, now? Besides, anybody else but you would have realized it long before this." She hiccuped.

His eyes widened. "Oh, is that so?"

Jennifer took the bandanna off her head and mopped her cheeks with it. "Yes, that's so."

He took the kerchief from her and finished the job. "Perhaps you'll be kind enough to tell me how I was supposed to detect your mad passion for me when you were throwing me out of your apartment. This was followed, as I recall, by your packing up and moving 1,300 miles away without even a good-bye. I emerged from the hospital to find that you had vanished."

"After you convinced me there was no future for us."

Lee dropped his eyes. "Forgive me, Jen. I was wrong. I had a lot of time to think while I was laid up, to reevaluate everything. I guess the scare made me realize what really mattered to me." He paused. "Joe and Dawn told me how you came to the hospital." He looked up again. "Nothing is as important as you and me, and our love."

"Are you sure, Lee? I know what your roots mean to you."

"I'm sure. I guess I finally see that having you doesn't mean that I have to give them up. Don't you think we can work it out?"

"I haven't been able to think since I opened that door and saw you."

He knelt before her and took her tenderly in his arms. She sought his mouth blindly with hers.

A long while later he said, "There won't be as much money, with me in school, but I've saved quite a bit, and the condo and the car are free and clear. We can live in the condo after we're married, if you like, it's only forty minutes to the school from there, and I'm sure Harry will take you back at the Freedom, that is, if you want to work . . ." He hesitated. "And I'd like you to think about going back to Montana with me after I finish school. It'll be our decision, of course, but please say you'll consider it."

Jennifer smiled. "Could they use another lawyer in Cawassa, Montana?"

Lee hugged her tighter. "In Cawassa, Montana, they could use another everything." He drew back to look at her. Something was wrong. "Jennifer, what is it?"

"Nothing."

But he knew. "The hell with your ex-husband, may he crash and burn and dwell in Hades forever." He turned her to face him. "I'm not *him,* honey. Just because your first marriage was a disaster, doesn't mean ours will be." He pressed her face against his shoulder. "Indians are loyal, don't you know that? Loyal, brave, thrifty, clean, and reverent."

"I think you're talking about the Boy Scouts," Jennifer mumbled into his sweater.

"Same thing," he said above her head. "Indians, Scouts, Indian scouts. I can see that you were never a fan of 'Wagon Train.'"

She clutched him tighter, wanting desperately to believe. "Lee, I hope you've thought this out. It's a lot to handle, medical school, a new wife and . . ." She almost said baby, but caught herself in time.

"As long as you're with me, I can handle anything."

He picked her up and stretched her gently on the floor amidst the chaos, dropping next to her and cradling her in his arms, his hands roaming her body. Jennifer held her breath as he touched her rounded belly.

He chuckled. "We'd better put you on a diet, paleface. I think you're gaining weight." Then he seemed to freeze for a moment, recovering to sit up quickly and examine her more closely, lifting her shirt to take in the stretch bra and the elastic waist of her pants. She saw the realization dawn on his face.

"It's mine," he said wonderingly.

Jennifer punched him. "Baboon. Who else could it belong to?"

He hugged her to him fiercely, saying in a strangled voice, "You'd better stop calling me names, paleface, or I might forget that you're supposed to be crazy about me." He set her down again and slid along the floor to press his cheek against her belly, his eyes closing luxuriously. Jennifer caressed his soft hair, holding his head, too full to speak.

"When?" he asked hoarsely.

"May."

He smiled. "That first time. I knew it, I felt it, even then."

Jennifer was amused. "Oh, really?"

Color seeped into his face. "I meant, I knew we had . . . set some force in motion. About this . . . well, I guess I thought you would take care of it."

Typical male, Jennifer thought. "Wrong again, Beaufort."

"Oh."

She sat up. "You know, that's really an insult. Assuming that I would just be prepared under any circumstances. I was living alone when I met you, and I wasn't exactly entertaining the Eighth Army on a regular basis. And our first encounter was, uh, rather spontaneous, if you recall."

"I recall. Spontaneous as in combustion. I felt like I'd been hit by a truck."

"Thanks a lot."

He kissed the tip of her nose. "Don't be dense, counselor. You know what I mean." He smiled and sang softly, " 'What a lady, what a night.' "

Now it was Jennifer's turn to blush.

He laughed. "Don't be embarrassed, little mother. I'm looking forward to many more of the same." He cupped her chin in both of his hands and looked into her eyes. "I can't believe you weren't going to tell me."

Jennifer shook her head. "I didn't want to get you that way."

He looked away. "But you didn't have to go through with it. You could have—"

"No," Jennifer interrupted him, not letting him finish the thought. "I love you, Lee. I wanted your baby. If I couldn't have you, then I wanted *something* of yours to keep."

He turned aside, blinking rapidly and brushing his eyes with the back of his arm. "That settles it," he said firmly. "We're getting married in ten minutes."

Jennifer giggled. "I don't think so, Lee. There are licenses, and blood tests, and things."

"Well, then, as soon as possible." He drew her to him swiftly. "And in the meantime," he murmured, unbuttoning her overblouse, "we'll have to think of something to do."

"Any ideas?" Jennifer said, sliding her hands under his sweater.

"I've got a few," he said thickly, and then stopped. "Is it all right? I mean, is it safe?"

Jennifer smiled indulgently and pressed into him, feeling his quick response. "Unless you plan on bursting into flames, or otherwise becoming a health hazard, it will be 'safe' for some time yet."

"Exactly what I wanted to hear," he said, taking off the rest of his clothes. "I don't suppose there would be such a thing as a bed?"

"I'm afraid not. It's in pieces in one of those boxes."

"Then we'll rough it," he responded, spreading his garments on the floor and pulling Jennifer down with him. "A man whose ancestors made do with packed dirt ought to be able to handle it," he added, nuzzling her. "God, you smell wonderful."

"You must be in love," Jennifer answered. "After the work I did today, I probably smell like the Freedom's locker room after a game."

"You know what?" he said, his words muffled by her flesh.

"What?" she groaned, arching under the touch of his lips.

"You talk too much."

And that was the end of the conversation.

Silhouette Desire

Six new titles are published on the first Friday every month. All are available at your local bookshop or newsagent, so make sure of obtaining your copies by taking note of the following dates:

APRIL 6th

MAY 4th

JUNE 1st

JULY 6th

AUGUST 3rd

SEPTEMBER 7th

Silhouette Desire

Coming Next Month

Image Of Love by Dixie Browning

How could Romany Caris convince Cameron
Sinclair that she meant business! Only after
the brief taste of happiness in his arms,
she wasn't sure she even wanted to.

Mountain Memory by Susanne Carey

Before the accident Kate McCullough had
planned to lure a reclusive film star back
to the movies. Now she only knew she
wanted to possess and be possessed
by this man named David.

Silent Beginnings by Ariel Berk

Widower Russell Van Doorn wanted the
best instructor money could buy. But when
he hired Kate Ryder he had no idea love
was part of the lesson.

Silhouette Desire

Coming Next Month

Winning Season by JoAnn Robbins

Just when Noel opened her heart to quarterback Ross McCormick she was offered a job in a different town. Should she leave the game at half time or try for a winning season with the man who'd touched her soul?

The Marrying Kind by Ashley Summers

Divorced and wary Jennifer decided that there was no room in her life for men—until she met Clint Forrest and he convinced her otherwise.

SummerSon by Angel Milan

When Ginger Holland was in Michael Merrick's masterful arms she was weak with desire. But how could she love a man whose dreams and lifestyle were totally opposite her own?

Silhouette Desire

THE MORE SENSUAL PROVOCATIVE ROMANCE

95p each

73 ☐ A KISS REMEMBERED
Erin St. Clare

74 ☐ BEYOND FANTASY
Billie Douglass

75 ☐ CHASE THE CLOUDS
Lindsay McKenna

76 ☐ STORMY SERENADE
Suzanne Michelle

77 ☐ SUMMER THUNDER
Elizabeth Lowell

78 ☐ BLUEPRINT FOR RAPTURE
Lenora Barber

79 ☐ SO SWEET A MADNESS
Suzanne Simms

80 ☐ FIRE AND ICE
Diana Palmer

81 ☐ OPENING BID
Marilyn Kennedy

82 ☐ SUMMER SONG
Rita Clay

83 ☐ HOME AT LAST
Sara Chance

84 ☐ IN A MOMENT'S TIME
Nora Powers

85 ☐ THE SILVER SNARE
Stephanie James

86 ☐ NATIVE SEASON'
Doreen Owens Malek

87 ☐ RECIPE FOR LOVE
Suzanne Michelle

88 ☐ WINGED VICTORY
June Trevor

89 ☐ TIME FOR TOMORROW
Erin Ross

90 ☐ WILD FLIGHT
Renee Roszel

All these books are available at your local bookshop or newsagent, or can be ordered direct from the publisher. Just tick the titles you want and fill in the form below.
Prices and availability subject to change without notice.

SILHOUETTE BOOKS, P.O. Box 11, Falmouth, Cornwall.

Please send cheque or postal order, and allow the following for postage and packing:

U.K. – 45p for one book, plus 20p for the second book, and 14p for each additional book ordered up to a £1.63 maximum.

B.F.P.O. and EIRE – 45p for the first book, plus 20p for the second book, and 14p per copy for the next 7 books, 8p per book thereafter.

OTHER OVERSEAS CUSTOMERS – 75p for the first book, plus 21p per copy for each additional book.

Name ....

Address ....

....